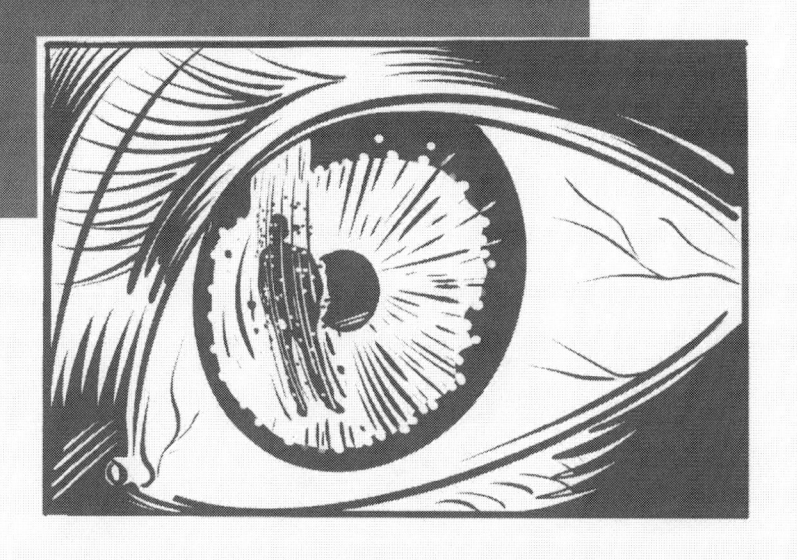

WINKED

A NOVEL

Ian Arco Cooper

Copyright © 2003 by Ian Cooper

All rights reserved.

No part of this publication may be reproduced, distributed, or transmitted in any form or by any means, including photocopying, recording, or other electronic or mechanical methods, without the prior written permission of the publisher, except as permitted by U.S. copyright law. For permission requests, contact [include publisher/author contact info].

The story, all names, characters, and incidents portrayed in this production are fictitious. No identification with actual persons (living or deceased), places, buildings, and products is intended or should be inferred.

Book Cover by Armando Valtierra

Contents

Dedication	IV
Foreword	V
1. Lax and Lad (1)	1
2. Lax and Lad (2)	16
3. Lax and Lad (3)	30
4. Lax and Lad (4)	48
5. Lad (5)	62
6. Victor Chambers (1)	71
7. Victor Chambers (2)	87
8. Victor Chambers (3)	103
9. Victor Chambers (4)	117
10. Justin Skay (1)	129
11. Justin Skay (2)	142
12. Justin Skay (3)	155
13. Justin Skay (4)	171
Also By Ian Arco Cooper	189

To my exceptional friends and family, your guidance turns my jumbled thoughts into something worth reading. A special thanks to my wife—the first line of defence against rogue commas and stray typos—I love you endlessly. Kudos to Amy for a top-notch edit, and a heartfelt shoutout to Scott and Shana for steering this story towards greatness or at least not-badness.

For my father, there are no words apart from love.

Foreword

Greetings, reader. You are about to delve into a narrative crafted to escape being trapped at home Written during a global COVID19 lockdown, this work explores themes of unfettered movement while I was paradoxically stuck in one place. I hope when you read you can feel the freedom I felt while writing.

This book seeks to raise questions about what true freedom of movement could mean to our world. How would things change with almost no borders or barriers? I felt the need to impose one major limitation on the freedom. I didn't want instant space travel to take over the story. So, I capped the speed of the tech below the speed of light, creating a narrative playground within our own galaxy.

The structure of this book offers the reader a choice. Presented through three unique perspectives, each story unfolds in a manner that allows you the freedom to choose your own path through the text. You may choose to read all the chapters sequentially (all the first chapters, then move on to all the second chapters, etc.) or follow each storyline to its individual conclusion...Just another bit freedom in the book.

Finally, it would be remiss not to extend my sincerest gratitude to you for choosing to invest your time in this book. The act of reading is a form of intellectual exploration, and for allowing me to be your guide on this particular journey, I am deeply thankful.

As you journey from Earth to Mars and from humble beginnings to transformative revolutions, it is my hope that you find this narrative as enlightening as it was for me to write.

Warmest regards,

Ian

Lax and Lad (1)

Dump and Run

IroncLad: "The human eye blinks in like a third of a second. A wink is way slower. Here look...that was like a full second."

LaxLuster: "I get that it's slower, that's not really the point. I'm just asking why it matters so much?"

IroncLad: "Dude, Lax! It matters because we're about to break the internet by sharing tech no one even knew was possible outside of the military. Life after this leak will be different, and we have a chance to set the name for the tech...now."

LaxLuster: "We're going to be famous either way. Hey, should we think about leaving the country before we drop the information?"

IroncLad: "Fine...I'm making the call. We're going to call it blink...blinking...'hey, I was feeling a little Genghis Khan so I blinked to Ulaanbaatar.' That feels right."

LaxLuster: "Honestly, dude, we need to figure out our escape plan, or we're gonna get fucked."

IroncLad: "How's this sound, we buy a couple tickets to Mongolia, they don't have an extradition treaty, we VPN in and drop the specs across as many sites as possible."

LaxLuster: "Two things, what the hell is with all the Mongolia junk today and where are we going to get the money to fly to Mongolia?"

In their mid-twenties, Chris Stevens and Alex Chen decided that it was more fun to play together than alone. They threw out a couple of names, which they meant to be temporary, and the handles stuck. Chris chose IroncLad and Alex opted for LaxLuster. They became Lax and Lad to the outside world as they made little bits of noise in the larger online community by trying small scale but cheeky hacks into corporate intranet sites in search of anything that made them laugh. Inappropriate emails and embarrassing HR problems were their bread and butter. They wrote a search algorithm that looked for a variety of key words to help them find their plunder. It was a hobby. They played at it just like they played video games. Which is to say, they joined forces in order to troll people, exploiting weaknesses and mistakes. They reveled in exposing people's true nature.

Neither realized the gravity of what they found when they managed to crack the password of a database administrator at a small defense contractor and stumbled on an email with an attachment. The attachment was large. Large attachments always drew their attention. Usually, big emails were just big data sets that were meaningless without context, but there were times where a large file size was the result of images or scanned content. This file was different. It was a large zipped file which was labeled as one of five. When they opened the file, they found CAD drawings that looked to be custom made for a very commonly used 3-D printer. Lax took a 3-D printing class at the local community college when he was still pretending to be the son his parents wanted, and he recognized the file types relatively quickly. He wasn't really sure what he was looking at, as the schematics were much more complex than anything he had seen in class, but he knew it was something more than their normal plunder of embarrassingly candid comments from executives or HR files revealing sexual harassment complaints.

When Lax first explained to Lad what he had found, they debated if it was worth dumping on the internet since it wasn't as obvious that there was a scandal.

Lax said, "we should at least check the other emails, maybe there's more meat in them. Besides I am sure someone will find this stuff interesting."

Lad agreed, and they continued to dig. They chased down the other 4 files and reviewed what they had. The nice engineers had left a description of the product that was clearly meant to help their higher-ups understand how they built the device. The description contained a few things that made Lax and Lad get wide eyed and maybe a little panicked:

"This file is classified as part of the On-Earth Instant Transfer Project as commissioned by DARPA."

"The attached G-code files are broken into the constituent pieces necessary to manufacture the entire system. Two copies must be made in order to create the loop."

"Each loop is a closed system allowing travel between nodes in less than a second which, while not representing greater than c travel, represents near instantaneous transfer of objects between any two points on a three-dimensional cartesian coordinate system where the destination point is mapped using the origin point as the relative point of reference."

"Theoretically, if a node's coordinates are known relative to the origin node, any node may be accessed from the origin."

It didn't take long for Lax and Lad to realize they had stumbled across some real-life science fiction, and the dreaming began. Here was an opportunity to cement their position as premier hackers within the community. What they had found was way beyond anything they had dug up in the past, even though they had tasted fame for their hacking in the past and enjoyed basking in their oddly anonymous fame. Their hacker names had been said on the news but still no one, no one that mattered at least, knew who they were in real life.

They had released sensitive information over the internet for years. Capture and release was their M.O. They called it dump and run. They would locate information and broadcast it to the world almost immediately then remain hidden behind the anonymity of their aliases. Some of what they leaked would get taken down too quickly to have an impact. Other information would get a life of its own. After playing catch and release with some low-level data for nearly a year, Lax and Lad found a juicy nugget they could release. They managed a social hack at a Hollywood talent agency which yielded tens of thousands of emails. Lax and Lad dropped the emails through Wikileaks and quickly claimed credit. The released emails almost instantly went viral. Lax's favorite email was an exchange between a talent agent and movie producer where the producer begged the agent to, "Kill me now if I have to sit through another reading with her. I mean, how can I rationalize making a giant bomb with her. Any fool could see it coming." The "her" in this case was a very famous, if sometimes flaky, actress who had pushed her way into the producers' movie. News stations broadcasted, comedians made jokes, celebrities were embarrassed and the two hackers tasted fame for the first time.

In the aftermath of the talent agency email dump, Lax and Lad reveled in their victory and vowed to always release hacked information as soon as they captured it. The point wasn't fortune. The point was infamy. A little fortune wouldn't hurt, but the infamy was truly glorious, and they had just stumbled upon something that would make them infamous around the world.

"I'm just digging on Mongolia since I streamed that Genghis Khan show on Netflix. I was looking shit up when it was on and found out they don't extradite. Seems important right now." Lad was hunched over his keyboard and his mouse hovering over the Wikileaks' secure submission link. He intended to use his well-worn release protocol that had served him well dozens of times before. Email a reporter or two they knew from their talent agency dump, load the files to Wikileaks, drop them on a dozen or so BitTorrent sites, and then email his listserv to quickly claim credit.

"Doesn't matter, there's no way we can leave the country. Let's just do the dump and run." Lax said, feeling his nerves fray.

"Dude, this is going to be huge. Make sure you call it Blink when you send the email over to the reporters. That name is going to kill."

"For sure. Let's do this. I'm hungry and I have to make an appearance at my parent's house tonight. They wanna talk about me going back to school. Something positive for the Chen family Christmas Card this year."

"Okay then. I'm hitting submit on Wikileaks now. You got your half of the torrents ready? Mine are."

"Of course, dude. Count it down?"

"5." The world wasn't ready for what was about to hit it.

"4." The two hackers weren't ready for it either.

"3." Almost no turning back now.

"2." A smile cracked on Lax's face. On a whim, he changed Blink to Wink in the email. It was going to piss Lad off something fierce. Once a troll, always a troll. Lax thought, "Man, I hope this shit goes viral so I can see Lad's face when they call it Wink."

"1." Boom.

***

The Chen household was an overly-typical American family unit. Mr. Chen was an account executive at a real estate services company and Mrs. Chen taught middle school STEM courses. They married after college, bought the requisite house and birthed the requisite two kids: Alex and Amelia who they called Amy for short. Amelia secretly wished they would have just named her Amy, if that is what they were going to call her all the time anyway. Amy was a track star and did theater. Alex was their "lazy" kid. He didn't really take to sports and didn't engage in extracurricular school activities, math club, or yearbook committees, but instead lived as much of his life as possible online.

Alex and Amy weren't close, but they weren't distant either. They were near enough in age but Alex's general aloofness kept Amy at a distance. They were different, but still family. Alex being very relaxed in tense situations infuriated the whole family. They would fight, Amy would yell but Alex would sit there not smiling, not frowning, just distracting himself with a paperclip or folding a sheet of paper that happened to be in front of him, so indifferent to her anger that it only made her angrier. Alex learned early that he could insight a riot in Amy by just relaxing while she raged. It was something he carried with him into his video games. His cool demeanor was a weapon. While his enemies broke down in frustration, Alex quipped and jabbed and pushed them over the edge using his relaxed wit. He had also become quite adept at absorbing his parents' frustration about his lack of drive and his "wasted talents."

Alex knew this visit with his parents was likely to be another in the string of conversations about his future and his plans, which were really their plans. To Alex, his parents weren't really interested in "his plans." They had a vision. He should follow it.

The Smart doorbell at the Chen's house picked up Alex's arrival and Mom and Dad met him at the front door with their usual hellos and quick hugs. There was always a formality when Alex saw his parents, they loved him, no doubt, but their expectations and mild disappointments colored their interactions. He wasn't where they wanted him to be in life, and there was a slight chilliness that had crept into their relationship as a result.

Dinner was delivered by a heavy set, clearly disenchanted Prius driver. Mr. Chen thanked her and gave a small tip. He never felt like deliveries deserved much in the way of tips. It's not like they were waiting tables and had to bring drinks and clean up. The driver gave a small smile that didn't extend to her eyes and slinked away back to her car.

Mrs. Chen had set out plates and the family sat down to eat. Alex knew the college conversation was about to start. Amy clearly knew as well, having already pulled out her cell phone and set it on the table for the inevitable moment where her attention wasn't needed. The food was decent, but lost flavor for Alex as his parents began their discussion of goals.

"Honey, have you given any more thought to the coding academy that Bob Jenkins runs at Tipton Community College? He says the placement rates are really high and the salaries are pretty good. It might be good to get the piece of paper to prove you can do what you already know how to do." Mrs. Chen started the volley.

"Yeah, I thought about it. I'm just not sure yet." Alex put some more food in his mouth to make it seem like he couldn't continue talking.

"You need to really do more than think. You are getting to an age where it's going to get harder and harder to get your education. Amy, can you stop your phone from buzzing on the table?" Mr. Chen said without actually looking over at Amy. His gaze was still fixed on Alex.

"Sorry, dad." Amy hit the button on the side of her phone, and a moment later it buzzed again.

"People go to school whenever now. It's not a big deal anymore," said Alex.

"That's not really the point. You aren't really doing what you could be doing. You have potential. Your father and I both see it. You can do so much more than you already are. Seriously, Amy, shut that off. Is there an Amber Alert or something?" Mr. Chen waved his fork back and forth with his elbow resting on the table.

"Let me look." Amy lifted her phone off the table, let it scan her face and unlock. Her face changed. Not a smile, but not a frown. She seemed frozen between awe and laughter. "Alex, what did you do?!"

"What are you talking about?" Alex still didn't lift his head from his food. Though he had a suspicion that the day's earlier escapades got some attention. Maybe he should have listened to Lad about the impact of their data dump.

"I just got like 20 texts. They're saying you're on the news."

Mrs. Chen stood up and walked to the television. She grabbed the remote from the TV stand and quickly flipped to a 24-hour news network. A commercial for an irritable bowel syndrome drug was on. The whole family was now waiting at the table, not eating and staring at the TV in the living room. When the news finally came on, a reporter began talking about a recent political gaffe made by a senator from West Virginia. The crawl at the bottom of the screen told a very different story.

Alex had kept his hacker alias mostly a secret, though he really couldn't resist telling his sister about his celebrity email leak when Amy was bragging about a race she had recently dominated. Her gloating was too much and he had to try to knock her down a peg. It didn't really work. She barely reacted which made Alex think she didn't believe him, but it was just her choosing to not let him win.

It wasn't until Amy shared his hacker identity with some friends that Alex realized she believed him. She used his exploits to play her own game of one-up with her friends. He should've been smarter than sharing his handle with Amy. She was never one to keep his secrets when she could score a point or two in a conversation. Alex slipped once, he let Amy get to him and now he was really regretting it. When he looked over to Amy, he knew his fate was sealed and it crushed him. She smiled and he slumped in his seat with a hangdog expression on his face.

"Breaking news: Top secret DARPA technology plans released on the internet. Two hackers claim credit. LaxLuster and IroncLad made news a year ago with their release of emails acquired from the talent agency Benson Media group. Their most recent release contained plans for a device that was under development at DARPA. The technology seems to allow for Star Trek-like teleportation using parts that are 3-D printable."

Amy's chair squeaked against the floor as she rotated on the spot to face Alex again, who was now staring blankly at the crawl, slack-jawed, and eyes wide open. "Alex! What the hell? Did you really hack top secret information?"

"I'm confused. Amy, are you saying your brother is one of those hackers? Alex, is that true?" Mrs. Chen leveled her gaze on Alex like a cartoon anvil dropping on Bugs' head. Her words had a sharp edge to them and Alex was clearly shaken. Mrs. Chen could see it, but wasn't interested in lightening up. She decided to double down on her anger when Alex didn't respond immediately. "Alex! Answer me. What is going on?"

Alex's default setting was snark. All those years of practice trolling on the internet, in games, and in person (where possible) had led to this moment. Alex brought his face back to his normal mild, mostly disinterested aspect and said to his mother and father. "Nothing too big. Hey, can I borrow some money for a flight? I really want to check out Mongolia".

Alex's parents spent the next few hours engaging in hard-core parental probing. Alex was doing his best to keep his parents at a distance by sharing as little information as possible which had the predictable outcome of driving them crazy. Alex wasn't really interested in his parent's input about his hacking work. Mostly, he wanted the conversation to be over so he could connect with Chris and get moving on whatever they were going to do next. The Chen's had to pull the information out of him piece by piece. Mr. and Mrs. Chen were lucky to have Amy home for the conversation. She was able to speed things up a bit by spilling all of her beans. She told mom and dad about Alex's and Chris' previous hacks. It turns out she was aware of a lot more than just the Benson hack. She must have been listening to conversations for a while.

When the story was finally all told there was a few minutes of silence. Alex broke the quiet with, "So...how about that trip to Mongolia?" He said it jokingly but was on the level in terms of his need for cash. Mongolia still seemed like a silly plan, but given how quickly things were moving, it was the only option that came to him.

Mrs. Chen and Mr. Chen exchanged glances. "Should we talk in the kitchen?" That was Chen household code for a fight between parents. Mr. and Mrs. Chen had always been able to keep their fights out of sight of their kids. This occasion wasn't enough to break the old habits. They stood up from the table, Mrs. Chen grabbed a few plates and brought them to the kitchen with her. When the tink of the dishes in the sink stopped, the conversation between the Chen's began.

On the other side of the kitchen door, Amy and Alex were sitting in silence listening to the occasional muffled but clearly raised voices and watching the television as the news continued to flow. "A spokesperson for DARPA director Dr. Torrence Jackson has released a statement regarding the recent hack, warning citizens who come across the leaked plans to avoid attempting to synthesize the designs as they are dangerous and untested. The spokesperson also noted that the Department of Defense would be seeking and prosecuting the two hackers, IroncLad and LaxLuster." The reporter smiled and said directly into the camera. "I am sure asking everyone to avoid looking into Pandora's box will work."

Alex smiled at the bit of wit coming from the typically stayed newscaster. He loved hearing his handle said out loud on the news, though he was worried his real name would be available to the public pretty quickly, especially with how loose lipped Amy had been. He and Lad needed to get somewhere safe in a hurry. He looked over at Amy who looked pale and a little sick. "What's up with you?"

"I'm sorry Alex. I just realized there's no way your name is going to stay secret very long. You are really screwed." Amy paused and contemplated her next move. She resigned herself to making things right. "I have some money in my account. How much do you need to get somewhere safe?"

"Honestly, I haven't looked into it yet. I probably should, though. It's odd that Chris hasn't called yet. He was expecting all this shit." A bolt of lightning hit Alex as he realized the problem. "Wait, where's my phone?" Alex patted down his pockets and came up empty-handed. "Guaranteed I left it in the car. Be right back." He stood up and went out the front door at speed. When the door shut behind him, he heard his parents say his name loudly in the living room. At that moment, Alex seriously considered running before he had to hear from his parents. He wasn't really sure why. They'd always been good to him, and he was sure they would try to help. He guessed he just didn't want to deal with them right now. He wanted to find Lad and make a plan. He opened the door and sat in the driver's seat, grabbed his phone off the center console, and fiddled in his pocket for his keys.

There was a tap on the passenger window that sent Alex's dinner up his throat and started his heart beating at a whole new level. It sounded like a cop tapping on the glass with one of their flashlights. Time practically stopped for Alex. It seemed like he had an eternity to make his decision. He hung his head, reached for the door handle, opened the driver side door and turned at his waist so his feet were out the door. He was waiting for the inevitable cop announcement to put his hands on the hood of the car. Instead, Lad said, "Dude, we need to get the hell out of here. I got us two tickets to Mongolia for real. God, that sounds ridiculous. You know that sounds ridiculous, right? Do you have anything here you can pack to travel? We need to go now."

Alex was too stunned to talk.

"Also, bro...I heard them say Wink on the radio on my way here. What the hell?!" That managed to snap Alex out of his stupor and brought a wry smile to his face, but before he could quip his parents were out the door and ushering him and Chris back into the house.

They all sat on the two couches in the living room and Mrs. Chen offered dinner to Chris, though the timing seemed wrong. Chris declined. He was in no mood to eat. Anxiety had taken him over. He was always one to think through every detail. Chris ruminated, thought about how much he was obsessing about things and then obsessed about his obsession. It was a cycle that was all too common for him. Truth be told, the rumination was what made him such a good coder. He could obsess over the details and find elegant solutions and write clean code as a result.

"Chris and I need to talk. We are going to head out. I'll call you guys later." Alex said shortly after sitting down. He didn't want to prolong the visit anymore. He knew Chris would be itching to get out of there and if he really bought tickets to Mongolia, they were probably for a flight leaving shortly. It did beg the question, where did Chris get the money? In his earlier Mongolian daydream Alex had checked on flights and they were expensive. Even when he put in dates months out, the flights were around $1,000 each way not to mention the crazy travel time, 64 hours. Most had connecting flights in places like Seoul or various cities in China. The whole idea of going to Mongolia sounded absolutely out of the realm of possibility. The only saving grace was that Lax and Lad both had passports ready from a trip down to Mexico.

"You aren't going anywhere until we talk about this situation," said Mr. Chen. Chris shifted on his cushion and shoved his hands under his legs. Alex flopped back on the couch and got into a relaxed but ready position for the oncoming fight.

"Fine, what do you want to talk about?"

"Let's start with the whole story, and be honest. It sounds like this is a big deal, and we can't help if we don't understand." Mrs. Chen's lip quivered a little at the tail end of the sentence. She was holding herself together, if only barely.

"Fine! Chris, you tell them." Alex grabbed his phone and started to scroll. He wanted to do a little more research on Mongolia before he became a resident. Chris told the story of their hack and release of the information with enthusiasm, though his voice and hands were shaking, and his heartbeat was visible in his neck. He ended up not hearing from Alex and getting worried. So, Chris headed for the Chen's house knowing they had dinner plans and hoping they were here.

At the end of the tale the Chen's looked exhausted. Alex could hear the what-were-you-thinkings bouncing around in both his parents' heads. They looked at each other and confirmed.

"Here's the deal," started Mr. Chen, "What you did was stupid, no doubt, but now doesn't seem like the time to work through that. Your mother and I already agreed that we are pissed off, and will be sure to give you the full rundown of our disappointment later." His sigh was like releasing the tension from his body. "Right now, we need to worry about your safety. If the newscasters are right, the government is going to come for you, and they will likely find you. So, now we want to know what you are planning."

Chris jumped in without a beat. "I already bought two tickets to Mongolia that leave in..." He turned his wrist to check a watch that wasn't really there, "like three hours from now. We really should go. We can't miss the flight. I have a bag in my car. Alex, can you grab anything here?"

"Where will you stay? How will you pay for it? Don't you need shots or something? Why the hell did you pick Mongolia? Have you even given this *any* thought? Honestly, you didn't even discuss what would happen before you leaked this shit." Mr. Chen was working himself up into a tornado. He stood up, knocked the coffee table hard, swore again, and rounded on Alex. "Well?!"

"We talked a little." Alex knew the one or two sentences of discussion right before dropping the data didn't really qualify, but he wasn't about to share that with his parents.

"Mongolia has no extradition. I found a hotel that was cheap. We'll just take a cab when we get there." Chris, of course, had already started to work through the details. "I have a little money in my account. It should last a few days at least. Then we will have to figure something else out."

"Figure something else out..." Mr. Chen said with as much disdain in his voice as he could muster. "Honey, can you go upstairs and see what clothes we can throw in a bag for Tweedle-dee and Tweedle-couldn't-care-less here?" Mrs. Chen stood knowing she would cry the second she got to Alex's old bedroom closet to dig for clothes he had left there during various stays.

The sounds of Mrs. Chen rustling upstairs prompted Amy to get up and follow. The boys downstairs heard a faint, "Mom, are you okay," but they were too involved in Mr. Chen's oppressive glare to muster concern for Mrs. Chen.

"To business. Here's the deal. Your mom and I talked, and we are going to help you get out of the country even though neither of us like it. There are some strings. When you get to the hotel in Mongolia you are going to call and let us know you are there and safe. You are also going to talk to a lawyer." Mr. Chen noticed Alex about to object and quickly added," We'll find one for you. You are also going to repay us for all of this. I'm going to run to the ATM and get as much cash as I can while you pack. This is a mess. Your mess, but I have a feeling the mess is going to spill over to us."

Chris noticed the silence after Mr. Chen's speech and got itchy. "Thanks Mr. Chen. We'll call you. I had my cell phone set up for international calls and data. I figured we need a translator on the phone." Mr. Chen walked to the door, opened it, paused and walked out, all the while looking at Alex.

Lax and Lad took the opportunity to go upstairs and rummage for supplies. Alex hugged his mom while she helped him pack. Amy watched the commotion and let out tears of guilt having realized her loose lips made Alex and Chris vulnerable. She reached out and hugged her brother and apologized. They managed to scrounge four days' worth of outerwear but underwear was in short supply. Plundering the bathroom yielded a couple toothbrushes, some toothpaste, a few safety razors (which both boys thought would be unlikely to get used), two sticks of deodorant (one pH balanced for women), and a small pile of pills. A mostly empty Tylenol bottle became Mrs. Chen's drug mule. To it, she added allergy medicine, cold medicine, a sneaky couple of Xanax from her private stash and what she guessed would be the most used pill, some anti-diarrheals.

Mr. Chen returned with $500 in cash which he added to an extra $136 they had laying around the house and gave it to Alex. He also added in his American Express card and told Alex to only use it if he was in serious trouble. The family gathered around the front door as the moment of departure neared. The bags were packed, the money was given, and all that was left was the act of leaving. They had called a ride share service to take the boys to the airport, since they didn't want Alex or Chris' cars to reside in an impound lot permanently. The car was due in one minute, allowing only a gloriously short goodbye.

A few more hugs were exchanged, Chris was included, while the door remained open and the car waited at the curb. Alex told his parents they would be okay and not to worry. He said he would call as soon as they arrived in Mongolia. When he hugged his parents for the last time, he told each of them that he loved them and said he was sorry. One last wave and they were out the door and in the car. Finally, some time for the two of them to talk.

"Dude, where'd you get the money for the plane tickets and hotel and shit?"

"I should have asked, man. I know. But I didn't see another choice." Lad shifted in the seat next to Lax, turning to face him in the dark of the back of the car. "Do you remember that reporter that sent us her information after we did the Benson dump? I called her. I had to promise to give her our first exclusive. She sent $15,000."

"No shit?! That's a lot. Why didn't you say something at my parents'? We didn't need to take all that money from them."

"If what she said on the phone is right, we're probably going to need all the money we can get."

Lax and Lad (2)

------

15 Minutes of Fame

"What would you say to critics who say that you are nothing more than digital paparazzi, but worse? That you don't seem to care how the content you release impacts the world around you?"

There was the normal pause for the distance delay between New York and Mongolia. While the question was in transit the camera was still, showing what was obviously a hotel room. Sheer white curtains hung behind the blocky but thin looking human figure which was centered for the camera. He was sitting on a standard fabric and wood low back chair. The kind of chair which populates almost all hotel rooms that have a table. The room was small. A particularly sharp-eyed member of the audience might have noticed that there wasn't much space between the chair and the curtains and that the figure filled up a lot of the camera frame, hinting that there was barely enough room to film in the small space.

The response to the question finally came. The voice on the other end was deep and robotic from being disguised. "I guess I would say, I get it. I don't know though; the American people pay for the research DARPA does. Don't we have any right to what they create? I mean, this is technology - not spy stuff. Still, I get the problems."

"'Problems' is right. There are a ton of problems. The United States had an immigration problem before the Winking technology got out. We had trouble controlling drug trafficking until Winking made control impossible. Aren't you and your partner LaxLuster responsible for our new inability to control our borders?"

"I wouldn't say we are responsible. It's not like there weren't immigrants before. At least they don't have to die to get into the U.S. now. There have always been drugs in America too. Shouldn't it be fixed on the demand side, not the supply side." Lad had pulled that little nugget off a more liberal website he read earlier that day. At least not everyone was blaming him and Alex for all the problems of the country. He knew he was in for this kind of conversation, after all they signed a deal with a conservative news network. The government had banned the creation of Winking devices using the leaked schematics and was waging a public campaign against Winking as unsafe, untested.

Alex and Chris had been watching a lot of news together lately. Especially late at night (or early in the morning) as they fell asleep in their matching queen beds, placed only two feet apart. Those nights felt just like they had when they had sleepovers at 10 years old. That sense of breaking the rules was all around them. The conversations didn't sound that different either. "Hey Alex, if you could get out of here and go anywhere, where would you go?" The two had really never been as close as they were during their "hiding out." It would be hard to be much closer. They were together all day, every day. They hadn't seen Mongolia. What they did manage to do was hide in a place where they had daily trouble communicating with anyone in the outside world. Sometimes it was miserable.

"What a cop out. You are safe, wherever you are, not worried about your job being lost to an immigrant or your kids being exposed to drugs at school like never before. You must have seen this coming. The government had the technology listed as top secret for a reason." The reporter was escalating. Chris knew it. These are the times he would rather have Alex talking. Alex would have just shrugged and given the reporter nothing and then delighted in watching her squirm and rage. As it was, Chris was starting to feel his heat rising. His palms started sweating hours before the interviews, and they didn't stop for hours after. He hated doing them, but they needed the money. The lawyers weren't cheap.

"Honestly, we didn't really know what we had. We knew it could be made on 3-D printers, but we had no idea that it would make it possible for people to just pop up anywhere on the planet any time."

"If you knew, would you have done things differently?"

"Probably. I mean we still would have dumped the files, but we probably would have planned better. I haven't seen a girl that wasn't on a screen in over six months now. Lad is cool but a guy's got needs." Chris immediately regretted saying that. He knew that was going to be all over their social media in five minutes. There would be offers, and there would be ridicule.

"Pardon me, if I don't feel bad for you."

The interrogation was over after another 5 minutes. The interview was painful for Chris, but at least it broke up the monotony. Lax and Lad's lawyers, which they had a team of now, had told them to stay in their room or they would risk getting "intercepted." The two were sufficiently scared and chose to stay on total lockdown. They ordered food to their room. Their parents sent care packages fairly often, and there were always video calls.

Six months had passed since the two hackers had fled home for Mongolia. They had passed through China to get there, which made them nervous. Chris had the good sense to buy the China to Mongolia leg of their trip through a Chinese airline directly, which bought them some space from prying U.S. government officials. The lawyers had been in contact with the Defense Department and the FBI, who were well aware of Lax and Lad's real names. The only reasons the two departments didn't release the information to the public was to avoid increasing the hackers' notoriety and to protect Alex and Chris's families from a media blitz which would likely result in death threats for which the FBI would be obligated to provide a protection detail.

Alex was sitting on his bed with headphones on, staring at his computer. There was the periodic ticking of keys on his laptop, the sounds of street noises outside, and the smell of food coming down the hallway. The 12-hour time difference between New York and Ulaanbaatar left only a few convenient interview times. In this case it was 7:00 a.m. (p.m. for New Yorkers), before the two had breakfast. Now that the nerves were wearing off, Chris was starving. He grabbed the phone next to his bed and ordered the breakfast they had most mornings, bacon, eggs and toast. While they had sampled other items from the buffet in the lobby area, particularly traditional curdled milk, in the end, the comfort of normalcy won out and the two reverted to their normal eating habits. They were both gaining weight. Sitting in a room all day and ordering food for every meal added pounds relatively quickly, even though Lax and Lad were both thin to start with. The two friends ate every meal together and made an effort to turn off all media and just talk and eat.

When the food arrived, Alex put away his laptop and Chris turned off the television. They sat at the small, two-toned wooden table at the foot of Chris's bed. They opened the window onto the patio for fresh air while they ate. The air was brisk. It had to be below freezing outside, but the room was humid and the cold breeze felt nice in the morning. It was a good way to wake up.

"How was the interview?"

"You really didn't listen?"

"Nah. I'm tired of them." Alex brought a forkful of egg to his mouth.

"It was normal. I did get to use that line about 'solving the demand problem', but I don't think the reporter was even listening, though. She was blaming us for the illegal immigration and drugs that were coming through the Wink units." Chris' turn to take a bite.

"No surprise there. That channel is full of assholes. How're we doing on cash? I got another email about a book deal. Is it time to sign up?"

"We're good for another few months at least. I say we hold out. I don't care what the government says, there is no way people are going to stay away from Winking. It's too choice." Chris set his fork down and leaned in. "Do you think we could print one here if we ordered the right gear? We could Wink home and get a pizza."

"Who would print one on the other side for us to land on? Not my parents. They're still scared shitless."

"There are all the fans online, someone is bound to play ball."

"You trust that shit? I don't. We don't know who's a narc, and who isn't." Alex took a bite of the crispy bacon.

"Guess you're right. Do you think this shit is all our fault? I mean, we kinda got screwed here."

"Nah. It would have come out at some point. We just sped it up and made sure the tech didn't get stuck in the hands of the corporate dicks. Just relax, it will blow over at some point. We can cash in a little along the way and head home once our lawyers give the 'all clear.' What did they say last time we talked...something about a few months in minimum security. Sounds doable at this point. I mean how different can it be from being stuck in this shit stack?" Alex waived a hand at their tight quarters. The room was surprisingly tidy considering two young men were in it nearly all the time, but Alex had a sneaking suspicion that it smelled ripe and they had just gone nose blind to their stink. He saw the bellman's face when Chris opened the door for the food. There was no mistaking that expression.

"Alright. Well, I'm going to sign up for the hacker interview on Project Zorak's YouTube channel. They didn't offer much money, $500, but I want to talk to someone friendly. Plus, it will be cool to get into the comments after the video posts."

"Sounds good. What do you want to do with the rest of the day?" This was a daily conversation for the two. They didn't dare do any hacking, and the internet connection wasn't really up to online game play. They figured out they could hijack the cat5 cable in their room to set up a LAN and play games together. That killed a fair number of hours. They would download games overnight and play all day sometimes. Other times, Lax would drive Lad crazy when they played. They were on a break because they nearly got into a fist fight last time they played. It would be more accurate to say Lad nearly punched Lax in the face for being so Lax.

Chris leaned back slightly, there was only an inch available for his chair. He lifted the front legs off the ground just a little and bumped into the wall behind him. He thought for a few seconds and came up with an option. "How about we start something?"

"Might need a little more than that."

"I keep thinking we're getting nothing but bad press. We should make some noise about the good that could come from Winking. Might help our case in the long run. I want to talk about the possibilities in the Zorak interview. Whadda you think?" Chris was expecting to get shot down. Alex seemed to shy away any time Chris talked about Winking. He didn't mind talking about the hack, but he didn't seem to be interested in talking about the technology itself. "I'm thinking we ask hackers to do good with the Winking units. We just need to tell them we are bucking the government who's trying to keep the technology locked down and give them some options to work with. I was hoping you'd sit with me this afternoon and work out a few suggestions."

"I don't know. Aren't you worried about making all of this worse?"

"Not really. I mean how much worse can we make it? The shit's out there. The government will never get the plans off the internet. At this point, other governments are using the designs to make their own tech. I want the control to be in the hands of regular people, not shitty government agencies who will use it for shitty things."

"Jesus, when did you get so political?"

"Dude, I'm not. I just want something better to talk about in the interviews. That's all." Chris flopped his hand on the table, not intending to slam them down, but definitely dropping them harder than he intended. He startled himself and definitely got Alex's attention.

Alex looked up, eyes wide and said, "Okay...Okay! If it's that important to you, let's do it." Chris decided not to mention the hand slam was an accident since it got the desired outcome. The two ended up talking for a couple hours and made a plan for the interview. They would both join the interview as Lax and Lad and send out a message to the larger community.

...

YouTube Channel interviews were different from the formal newscaster interviews. Gone were the fancy camera equipment and preparation sessions in favor of cell phones with face blur and voice changing apps. The camera quality wasn't as good, but it didn't really seem to change the quality of the conversations. The questions from the Youtubers tended to be more fun and less combative. More like talking to friends, which could be disarming. Even when he was on his guard Lad found himself saying things he didn't intend, it was worse when things were less formal. This interview would be different though, he thought. This one he had planned with Alex. Lad knew what he wanted to say and he was ready and his partner would be there with him to step in if things started to go sideways. Lax and Lad always made a good team and even more so now that they were essentially a married couple.

The producer of Project Zorak, who was just a buddy of the host, had asked Lax and Lad to log in five minutes early since they would be livestreaming the interview. The producer had mentioned they expected an "epic" turnout given the feedback they had been getting. Lad insisted they get on the video call ten minutes early; he was clearly excited at the prospect of taking control of the story. He wanted to get his spin out to the public, and both Lax and Lad were confident they had come up with some compelling talking points, though Alex never came out and said so.

"Nice! You guys are already on. I was just making sure the mics and camera are working on this side, but we can check yours too. Are you guys ready for the interview?"

"For sure! We have a few things we want to say," Chris said.

"Can you confirm we are blurred and the voice changer is working?" Alex played counterbalance to Chris' enthusiasm.

"You are all good. You sound like robots with deep voices and look like a 1980's video game."

"Thanks, we need to be careful." Chris jumped in.

"For sure! I get it. It's going to be awesome to have LaxLuster and IroncLad on this show. It's a pretty big get for us. You guys are super famous now." The producer seemed to be playing the fanboy role well, or maybe he really did look at them as celebrities. The thought seemed crazy to Chris. "Okay, which one is Lax and which is Lad? Oh, and is it cool if we just call you Lax and Lad?"

Chris identified them both for the producer and told the producer they actually preferred Lax and Lad lately. It was a happy coincidence that their names worked so well together.

A few minutes later, the host, who went by the name Silverberg, joined the call. He greeted the two, got their position in camera down and asked if they had anything special, they wanted to talk about during the show.

"Definitely. We kind of have some prepared remarks. Is that okay?" Chris asked.

"For sure. You want to say them at the beginning or end?"

"Beginning. Maybe right after the intro?"

"That works. Here we go then. Show time." The livestream icon flashed to red. In a few heartbeats, Silverberg started his intro over the Zorak graphic which was clearly hijacked from Space Ghost Coast to Coast and altered for dramatic effect. "Welcome to everyone joining us for this livestream. I know a bunch of you are tuning in for the first time. This is Project Zorak, and we are joined by the infamous hacking duo LaxLuster and IroncLad, or as they are more commonly known these days, Lax and Lad. You probably know this but Lax and Lad are responsible for the hack and subsequent dump of Wink tech. Totally changed everything. The two would like to share some thoughts before we get into it. Lad, you're up man."

"Here's the deal. Technology isn't really bad or good. It's down to what people do with it. I've heard the same arguments for guns…'Guns don't kill people, people kill people,' but this is different. This technology has so many uses for good. Guns only kill. We get that right now the narrative is all negative. The Wink devices are pretty much only used, at least publicly, for things like trafficking and that feels bad, but the same could have been true for cars or planes. Imagine if cars were only ever used to carry booze during prohibition. Imagine if the government had told the public to stay away from cars because the tech was unproven and dangerous. The government could have been the only ones with cars. How would life be different? After all, cars kill a shitload of people every year, and we aren't trying to suppress them. We all recognize the good cars can bring to the world, but we also see the bad. Every technology, especially the new ones, is like that. Technology is always a mixed bag. We accept the inherent risks in the tools we use. Lax and I think Winking is no different. We also think the government has no right to suppress or limit the use of Winking. The hacker community comes together all the time to accomplish things we couldn't accomplish alone. Every DDoS attack, every coordinated attack we have made against organizations or people we see as threatening, unites us. We think this is one of those times."

"Whoa! What are you saying? You want some sort of new coordinated hack against, who, the whole U.S. Government?!" A bug-eyed Silverberg leaned into the camera.

"No, what Lad is saying is that we need a coordinated effort to show the world the good Winking can bring."

"Yeah, I'm saying help us show the world what Winking can do for people who are in need. For example, getting food to needy communities around the world. With Winking you could hand groceries to someone hungry on the other side of the globe or give them clean water by stepping onto your portal and popping up on theirs. Cut greenhouse emissions. Set up a Winking unit in the office and have people Wink to work instead of driving. In fact, why do we even need cars? Sure, the tech isn't totally proven, but the drug dealers and human traffickers seem to be able to get it to work. So, why can't we? Lax and I sat down for a couple hours and came up with like fifty ways Winking could make life better, and we're just useless hackers. Help us make the list longer." Chris had been gesturing heavily with his hands and finally relaxed into a posture that said he was spent. He looked like a balloon with all the air let out.

"Well, shit." The papers in Silverberg's hand which must have contained his notes, flopped on the desk in front of him. His very subtle southern drawl was starting to come out as he let his guard down. "It's not what I meant to talk about, but... I was thinking of something the other night. My dad had to have a kidney transplant. He was stuck on a ridiculously long waiting list and was on dialysis for too long. It was miserable to watch. I read that there are willing 'living donors' in other parts of the world but there was no way for him to get there. He was too sick to really travel, his immune system was compromised and he really didn't have the money after paying all the medical bills. My dad was lucky because he got a transplant before he died, but lots of people aren't. Winking could have got him where he needed to be with no travel time and almost no cost. That's huge."

"Exactly. There are a million more examples. All we're asking is for our community to help this shit become real because right now the narrative is much different. Lax and I are the bad guys who unleashed Frankenstein's monster on the world and it's just going to wreck the place, but it turns out the monster's a pretty okay dude if we just took the time to get to know him. You know what I mean?"

"Dude, the live chat is lighting up. It sounds like we've all been thinking about it. Guess we just needed to let the monster out of the cage." Silverberg was clearly a little self-satisfied with his clever turn of phrase with what was clearly a new fan base.

The conversation went on for a while longer. They talked about the possibilities inherent in the Wink tech and a little bit about how Lax and Lad were faring. Neither complained, though Lax would have liked to. After the show, Silverberg asked if they wanted to do a debrief in a separate meeting space and hear about the livestream stats. Due to a previous mishap, he was always nervous about hanging out after a livestream in case they forgot to drop all the participants and ended up saying something unseemly in front of an audience.

The producer sent Lax and Lad a link through email. Lad was itching to hear the details.

"So, how'd it go? It's hard to get a read during the interview. I wanted to try to read the chat, but I know that's a mistake." Chris jumped on Silverberg and his producer immediately after Lax and Lad landed in the meeting space. Lad wasn't typically the self-conscious type, but he felt like their future was on the line. Unsurprisingly, Lax seemed pretty indifferent to the whole ordeal, but he would ride along with Lad. Even though he wasn't effusive, Lax was furiously loyal.

"It popped! There were just over 122,000 viewers. That's like ten times our most watched livestream. The chat was on fire too. It looks like there were around 1.5 million posts. Hey Tim, were you keeping up with it? What were people saying?" Silverberg threw it to the producer.

"Mostly, the posts were flying really fast. I'll get more details later, but my first impression was that people were supportive. The big volume of posts came when you asked people to think of the benefits of Winking. People were coming up with tons of stuff. Do you want me to send you the chatlog?"

"Hell yes! Anything stick out?" Chris probed.

"Just one thing for me but, I'm into space stuff. Someone pointed out we could drop a couple large units on the moon with a probe and send up supplies to make a moon base. We could have a working moon base in no time. I mean if you only have to launch and land one thing on the moon to get unlimited free access…the moon race is on, but this time it will be for real estate." Tim-the-producer smiled at his childlike glee, flashing himself back to reading H.G. Wells. Maybe he would go digging for gold like, "The First Me in the Moon." Tim thought they better make tunnels and call them mooncalves, or he would be really disappointed in humanity.

"That's sick! You are totally right. I can't wait to dig through the comments. I bet there's some hilarious shit in there."

"Thanks, Tim. I have to run, but you guys killed it today. We appreciate the lift. If you want to announce anything, don't forget about us. I'll send a check."

Silverberg was short and had lost his smile. Something seemed off, but Chris was on too much of a high to really worry about it. The meeting ended with Tim agreeing to send over all the data within the next couple days.

After a few days, things started to shift for Lax and Lad. Chris' impassioned speech had gone viral, largely because it was picked up by news sources all over the world and ran through pop culture in a hurry. The lawyers told the two their position was somewhat improved because they had gone on record and discussed their motivations. They were ready to argue the two hackers had no intent to harm the country, but rather to help the country and that the information released didn't in fact cause harm. If they could stay in Mongolia long enough for Winking to be leveraged for the good of Americans, the case would be significantly stronger. Sentencing guidelines for judges left a lot of leeway but maxed out at a likely ten-year prison sentence and a hefty fine. Both Alex and Chris deflated at the idea that they might have to spend the rest of their twenties and a little more in prison. Their faces told the story of their concerns, and the lawyers quickly responded with reassurances. Two of the major points the government had to prove in their case was malice of intent and actual harm. The lawyers would pitch, when the time was right, a case of positive intent and positive outcomes, hopefully reducing the sentence significantly. Still, the lawyers wanted to avoid Alex and Chris' identities being shared with the media. It was important that the two guys didn't seem like they were capitalizing on their fame. There would be time enough to write tell-all books and do the talk show circuits after the case settled. More isolation, more meals in the room, and more time as an old married couple was in store for the foreseeable future.

Chris' gambit showed all the signs of paying off over the next few months. Lax and Lad had become a rallying cry as people around the country started adding to the national conversation around the benefits of Winking. It was touted as a solution for income inequality since you could live anywhere and work anywhere. Winking would be the solution for global warming. Greenhouse gas emissions would go to near zero if everyone could just Wink from place to place. You could get food from anywhere, take a day trip to the Amazon

Jungle, and even balance the education of underprivileged students around the world. Lifting all the restrictions on travel time was going to change the world.

Winking devices were being printed all around the world by novices. Success abounded but so did failures. There were some reported cases of errors in the printing, but luckily when the devices were damaged, they ceased to function rather than creating horror stories of half Winked people who left an arm or leg at home while the rest of them went for a visit to Hawaii. It was still illegal, but it was becoming increasingly clear the government wouldn't be able to stop the distribution of the technology. There were just too many benefits of the tech. Imagine going to visit grandma in the old country every weekend for dinner or buying your first house in a state where the property values were still affordable.

Of course, not everything came up roses. There were cases where the receiving Winking unit was placed in a bad spot, and people paid the price. In one notable instance that made national headlines, a Florida man took his brother's receiving unit from his mom's house and placed it next to an alligator habitat. When the brother showed up to have dinner with mom, he found an unhappy gator on the other end who didn't appreciate the incursion on his turf. A bite to the leg sent the brother to the hospital and the local police were considering prosecution. There were instances of home invasions and robberies where people planted receiving devices where they were not welcome. Travel stocks took a nose dive in the market with airlines taking the biggest hit.

Lax and Lad watched the news constantly hoping for the good to outweigh the bad. The hacker community stepped up in a big way. They made sure the government couldn't take down the 3-D printer plans and encouraged Winking to be used for good. They leveraged coordinated hacker attacks on news agencies they saw as biased and punished corporations when they rallied against the tech because it threatened the status quo of their business model. It was just too soon to tell how things would play out.

The irony of their situation was obvious to both of them. They launched a technology that was accessible by anyone with access to a decent 3-D printer and would allow people to be anywhere on the planet in the Wink of an eye.

Winking meant untold freedom, and Alex and Chris couldn't get out of their hotel. They had trapped themselves by their choices. They chose to flee to where access to 3-D printers was extremely limited, a country where they didn't speak the language, where they had no friends and no real way of making friends with anyone other than the hotel staff. They were sure the United States Government knew where they were, which made them afraid to exit the hotel. They were trapped together in a prison of their own making.

Alex was increasingly morose about the Wink tech being seen as a force for good. He was also getting tired of being cooped up in a room with Chris. The two were fighting more. Alex had told Chris that he was a dreamer and was wasting his time hoping. He told Chris he was out the second he could figure a way to get out and that he would likely not see Chris again. The comments were said in anger. but Chris feared the truth behind the words. It was tension neither had experienced in their relationship before and while it would be obvious to Chris later that the fights were just a matter of stress, uncertainty and proximity, in the moment they seemed final. They both needed a little time apart. They both needed space.

Lax and Lad (3)

A Reckoning

"So, are you saying we should go back home?"

"I'm saying this might be the only reasonable window for you to try. The law seems to be on our side here. People can see more and more that a tremendous amount of good is possible with the Wink Tech. Each of you has made a strong case for your good intentions…that you leaked this tech in the interest of improving the quality of human existence. The legal test here is Mens Rea. It requires that you both had knowledge that you were doing wrong, and you intended to do that wrong when you released the information. If things start to go south with the Wink Tech for some reason, our case may not be as strong. As it stands today, I spoke with the FBI, and they agreed to a favorable sentencing recommendation if you turn yourselves in. I don't know for sure, but I am guessing 12 months for each of you in a minimum-security prison and maybe a small fine." There was a room of 4 lawyers on the other side of the video call who certainly looked the part. They were sitting at a large glossy wooden table in what looked like tailored suits. Every few minutes one of the lawyers would lean over to another lawyer and whisper something in the ear of his co-counsel. A curt nod was given and the conversation continued without skipping a beat.

On the Mongolian side of the call, two young men sat on an unmade bed in a hotel room, headboard in the background. They both had dark circles under their eyes and looked as though they hadn't seen sunlight for quite a while, which of course they hadn't. They had reversed course and were now thin due to their lack of interest in eating the same food every day and had both grown quiet and sullen. The two didn't lean and whisper to talk. They were way past that in their internment. Chris turned to Alex and saw his eyes. He'd lived with him long enough to know exactly what Alex was thinking. They had talked about it at great length. Alex would say, "What the hell is the difference between this jail cell and one back in the states? At least we could get some yard time."

"We're ready to go back. Can we negotiate which prison we go to? I did some research, and it looks like Otisville is the place to be." Chris had taken to doing all the talking. He and Alex would talk all night, but when they were on the phone with lawyers, or even news agencies at that point, Chris would handle the talking for them both. It had been quite a while since Alex disagreed with something Chris said. They were in sync.

"We can probably work something out. If you're both sure, we will get the details worked out over the next couple of days and book your travel. This is a big step guys, but we all agree it's the right one." There was general nodding on both sides of the call. "Would you like us to tell your parents or will you tell them?"

"We'll tell them. Can we break our return to the news agencies? It would make for a good interview and give us a little extra pocket money in case we have to pay a fine."

"Let us talk to the Justice Department and see if they would be explicitly against it. For now, hang tight, tell your parents, and start packing up. We'll call you tomorrow with news."

"Alright. Talk tomorrow." Chris waved; Alex didn't and the lawyers hung up.

Chris folded the laptop and shuffled to the dresser and set the laptop next to the TV where he plugged it in to charge. He sat back down at the edge of the bed, threw his arms up, and flopped backwards so his hand hit the pillows near the headboard. Alex was still sitting up, staring at the blank television screen.

Chris asked, "Should we bother packing any of this shit up? I'm tempted just to trash it all. I'm tired of looking at it."

"Yeah, we should toss it all. This place is a piece of shit. I can't wait to chill out in a prison cell. Kinda sounds like a vacation at this point," Alex said without turning or shifting his gaze from the powered down TV screen. "Can't wait to get some fresh air. I could walk around outside all day at this point, even if we have to watch our backs in the showers."

"Oooh yeah, sunlight sounds good," Chris said while looking at the ceiling. It was like he was looking into the sky trying to figure what shape the clouds made.

By the next day Lax and Lad had taken inventory of their rat's warren and each had small bags ready for the transit home. They joked about how neither really knew what would happen to the items they carried back with them. Was it like the movies? Were they going to have to strip down and hand over all their belongings to a prison guard on the other side of a metal barred window with a small slit in the bottom? Chris' imagination got to running wild and he pictured not having a cell at all, like in some of the shows he'd seen. They would be in the open, vulnerable. It felt impossibly naked compared to the claustrophobic room they'd lived in for so long. The hairs on his arms jumped at the thought and he shivered.

"You okay man?" Of course, Alex noticed the shiver.

"Yeah, just getting used to the idea of heading home," Chris replied.

Alex said, "Trading one rat hole for another. There's not too much to get used to in my book."

"No way we're going to be in the cell for long, at least if the lawyers are being straight up." Chris said, as they folded the few clothes they had and placed them on top of their other traveling belongings in their bags in an attempt to protect their stuff for travel, padding on top of the truly important items. The only exception would be their laptops, which would stay on top for easy access.

"What time are we supposed to be on with them again?" Asked Alex.

"They didn't say. We're supposed to wait for them to ca..." Chris whipped his head around at the sound of the phone ringing. "I swear to god, they're bugging us." Chris moved around the folding luggage rack he had pulled out of the closet and set it at the foot of his bed with his bag on top and picked up the hotel phone. "Hello."

"Chris? Is that you?"

"Dad! Hey, thought you were going to be with the lawyers. We got news. I was going to call and fill you in but hadn't got there yet."

"Actually, I talked to the lawyers earlier this morning, and they have a plan to bring you back. Did they tell you?"

"Yeah, we talked to them too and agreed to come back," Chris said, savoring the taste of coming home after nearly a year in Mongolia.

"That's good news. Your mom and I are excited to see you, but I called for something else. I got a call."

"Not a call..." Chris said sarcastically. Their relationship had fallen into a more informal mode since the info dump. Something about the weight of everything made them closer but also more like friends and less like father and son. It was like the gravity of what Chris and Alex had done had made them adults and closer to equals in his dad's eyes. Maybe it was a sign of respect or just that his parents realized they couldn't shape his life in the same way they used to and his parents settled into the idea that they were more sideline players.

"Yes, a call, but a serious one. The call was from Senator Sanderson. Do you know him?"

"Heard of him."

"You know he's running for president. He told me that he wanted to talk about pardoning you and Alex when he gets in office. He would like to make that a campaign pledge. I guess he thinks it'll be popular with young voters. Before he makes the announcement, he wants to see if he can get your support."

"What's that mean? We don't really do the politics thing."

"It means coming out publicly to support his reform platforms. He sees the Winking tech as a way to solve the global warming problem. He wants to lift the ban on the Wink tech and put it in the hands of big business for production under government safety regulations. He heard you and Alex talk about finding the benefits of the tech and thinks you struck a chord with the public. He wants to use it."

"It's that 'use it' shit we don't really like. His position should be his position. If it's good, people will vote for him. Why does he need me and Alex?"

"Sorry, I forgot, he told me to tell you 'he's old and when he talks about new tech, he sounds ridiculous.' He believes in you and Alex, and he believes in the tech. All he needs is for that to come through clearly to voters."

"That's pretty heavy. Let me talk to Alex. Should I call you and let you know what we decide?"

"There's no decision here. You take it. The pardon is a big deal for you two. No more being locked up. You need to take it. What's there to even consider?"

"Let me talk to Alex. I'll call you back." Chris hung up the phone before his dad could jump back in. He knew his dad would keep pushing until he agreed.

The conversation that night was new. During their many, many late nights, they had talked so many aspects of their lives to death. They talked about what it would be like to be home, what prison would be like, what they would do once they got out of prison. All the plans had them together the whole way. They would visit their parents together, be in the same cell in prison, get an apartment together after prison, and make money writing their book and doing talk shows together. They could probably make a nice living out of playing up the pseudo-celebrity bit for quite a while, if they did it right.

The conversation that night was more about their beliefs than it was about their future. It was deeper. They talked about how they felt about climate change; they agreed it sucked. They talked about how they felt about politics; they agreed it sucked. The conversation ping-ponged from what they knew about pardons to what they knew about Senator Sanderson. They didn't know much but they did trust their parents. While their parents seemed to have very different political views, Chris's were liberal and Alex's were conservative, both sets of parents were politically aware, if not active. Given the time difference, they were able to call Alex's parents first right after making their decision.

Alex's father was unequivocal. He and Alex's mother may not agree with Sanderson's politics, but the pardon was the way to go. Like it or not, and the Chen's did not, Sanderson was probably going to win. Their final decision was made quickly. They would support Sanderson, and if their math was right, they might get away with only a few months in prison.

***

Alex and Chris sat at the edges of their beds with their travel bags next to their legs. Chris's bag rested against his calf reminding him that their time in the hotel was almost over and the next phase of their lives was about to begin. Neither were talking as they waited for their escort and driver to knock on the door and herd them onto a plane back to America to "accept the consequences of their actions," as the lawyers had put it in their official agreement with the U.S. Government.

It took the lawyers only two weeks to work out a full deal with the government. Lax and Lad would travel back to the states in a plane chartered by the U.S. Government and then surrender themselves into custody where they would be processed and charged with theft of government property and disclosure of classified information. The two would plead guilty to the charges and sidestep any espionage or treason charges. They would then serve 6 months in the Otisville Federal Penitentiary. It was a reduced sentence. Apparently, Senator Sanderson still had some sway from his days as a lawyer, and he used that sway to land them where they wanted and for less time than Lax and Lad had expected. Also, they would be remanded to the custody of their parents during the trial, on house arrest with fancy ankle bracelets to boot. The lawyers said the trial should take a few weeks to clear. So, for a few weeks, other than court appearances the two boys would be able to sleep in a friendly bed, see other humans (even better, humans who genuinely cared about them), wander around in the backyard a bit, and find a sense of home again. Everything was planned. It was all autopilot from there until they left prison in, hopefully, less than six months because of their pardon.

Alex and Chris's parents were right about the pardon. It was a tremendous deal for them. Sanderson didn't expect much from them in exchange for the pardon. They would share a public statement prepared by a professional writer and approved by the Sanderson campaign and its cadre of lawyers and media analysts. There would be a speech, delivered by Chris of course, after which the two had agreed to stay quiet or on message until after the election. The conversation with Sanderson had made them both laugh for hours afterwards. Sanderson was a caricature of a southern politician, right down to the thick drawl, loud voice, and Foghorn Leghorn-like use of large words that never quite seemed to fit in the sentence correctly but somehow got the feeling right. Chris had settled on a favorite phrase pretty quickly. Sanderson said it while talking about the droughts in his home state of Texas and how climate change was making it: "so dry the trees are bribing the dogs." Great imagery. Alex's favorite was when Sanderson had apologized for being late to their phone meeting, only by a few minutes, though Sanderson made a point of saying tardiness was unbecoming of a southern gentleman. All the same, he had been, "Busy as a fart in a colander." Lax and Lad couldn't quite tell what that meant which led to a good hour of talking it through. Do the farts bounce around in the colander trying to find a way through? Who the hell is farting in a colander?

At the end of the call with Sanderson, Lax and Lad were big Sanderson fans. They understood why he was so popular. It's odd for someone in their early twenties to say so, but they both found him charming. Charming was the only word for it. During their late-night chat, they agreed they would have happily supported Sanderson even if he wasn't going to give them a pardon. The guy would have made a great salesman. Alex pointed out Sanderson was a salesman in his own way.

A knock on the door brought Lax and Lad back to attention. It was time for them to head to the airport and head home. The trip itself was surprisingly uneventful. They were driven to the airport with their minder, who didn't speak. The only conversation came from the driver. In heavily accented English he asked, "Are you enjoy-ed your time here?" His Rs rolled and he sounded like he might be singing. Chris responded with a polite, "It was very interesting," which seemed to meet the minimum conversation expectations and the conversation stopped. At the airport, they were shuffled up a set of stairs to a blue and white plane that had "United States of America" painted on the side and a United States flag on the tail. Neither Lax nor Lad had boarded a plane directly from the tarmac. It felt like a celebrity thing to do, and Chris toyed with the idea of stopping at the top to give a wave to no one in particular, but he thought better of it when he saw the armed guard at the top of the stairs. Inside the plane, the seats were large and black leather and further added to the feeling of being a celebrity. The captain gave a quick welcome aboard, and they took off.

Alex and Chris didn't really talk during the flight. They mostly stared out their small oval windows. Their seats were not next to each other, but were across an aisle which seemed to add more distance than the reality of the measurement. Adding to the distance were the quietly staring escorts on the plane. The plane didn't have the range to make it to the United States directly, so there was a stop in Japan to change planes. They exited one blue and white plane just to enter another blue and white plane, but with an older brown leather interior. Still, things were quiet as they traveled.

When they landed, they were at Andrews Airforce base in Maryland. The visual as they landed was of flat green earth and gray-brown concrete which was peppered with white planes. It could have been the same airport they left in Mongolia if it weren't for the contingent of police officers and lawyers waiting to see them off to holding and booking. They were read their Miranda rights when they stepped off the plane and placed in the back of what looked like a regular police car, but with FBI written on the side. The drive was relatively short and ended with being escorted into a building, up an elevator, and into a room that looked like a conference room. In the room they were photographed, fingerprinted, and told they would be staying in the room while they were processed and released to their parents' custody. Relief washed over Chris. He was anxious about being in jail; he had seen too many movies. The idea of going straight home with his parents lifted a weight that sat on his shoulders the whole trip back. Alex looked equally relieved.

 After all the booking details were complete, the Chens and Stevens were led into the conference room. The Stevens family embraced. Mrs. Stevens was all smiles while Mr. Stevens hugged Chris, pounded on his back and told Chris he was glad to have him home. Mrs. Chen cried and hugged Alex, then Mr. Chen heartily shook Alex's hand, a smile not quite cracking his face. After the greetings were over, Lax and Lad were fitted with new ankle monitors. They were non-descript gray plastic with a thick robust looking black band. The fit was surprisingly tight around their thin ankles. When Alex and Chris had discussed the eventuality of being tagged like wild animals in a research experiment, they had expected something to light up or beep periodically, but these monitors were kind of boring. The agents explained the conditions of the monitors, more to the parents than to Lax and Lad who were well into adulthood. The basic gist was, "don't leave the house, ever." The monitors would trigger if they left their parent's property and if they were removed or otherwise tampered with. Also, an automated system would be calling the house every day at random intervals to verify Alex and Chris were at home and an agent would likely be sent to periodically visit each house.

 Alex and Chris hadn't really connected the fact that they would be going to separate households. After so much time where it was just the two of them, a break wouldn't be the worst idea, but added a layer of anxiety for Chris.

 Chris spoke first after the monitor speech. "Are we allowed to talk on the phone and Skype interviews?"

 "You can talk on the phone or internet, but only to those on this list," a suited lawyer handed Chris a sheet of paper with a very limited list of names, but Chris was only really looking for one and Alex was on the list.

 "I don't see news agencies. Can we do interviews still? Can we use our real names and faces?" Chris asked.

"All requests for interviews are to be routed through your lawyers and will be vetted by the FBI before you can participate, but you can do interviews upon approval. We wouldn't want to violate your First Amendment right, would we?" The lawyer said this last phrase with thick sarcasm and a glance to one of the government lawyers. Clearly, interviews had been a bone of contention during the negotiations for the return of Lax and Lad.

"That works." Chris said and looked over at Alex who was staring off to the other side of the conference room. Alex looked done with the whole process. He just wanted to be home.

The families packed up and left the big room, with the lawyers still talking.

***

The next few weeks contained a series of firsts for Lax and Lad. For the first time, the hacker pair was unable to hack together, or even be in the same room. It was also the first time either had been to a courtroom or spoken to a judge. It was the first time they heard a recounting of what the Wink tech had been used for and who, specifically, was in charge of the tech, someone at DARPA named Victor Chambers.

Chambers was the managing director of the teleportation program at DARPA that had been unceremoniously nicknamed the "Forty Winks" program. The program was so named because the department had nearly 40 team members. After the specs for the Wink tech were released to the public by Lax and Lad and the name 'Wink' was adopted by the media, the team of 38 people decided on 40 winks. Chambers was an academic from the University of Chicago. He was a physicist by education and had been recruited by the Air Force for a study they were conducting on matter teleportation. Impressed by his organizational skills and technical knowledge, he was recruited to DARPA to head their teleportation division.

While on the stand during the sentencing portion of the hearings, Chambers presented as informal, an every-man sort. He made jokes on the stand and was self-effacing. Far from being a tweed jacket with elbow pads type, Chambers looked more like an older tech CEO. He was lean with short cropped salt and pepper hair. He wore dark skinny jeans and a gray t-shirt with a patterned blue blazer. He was comfortable and relaxed when speaking to the courtroom audience, but more importantly to Lax and Lad was the way he seemed to feel about the release of the Wink tech. It was clear he was upset about the systems being hacked but he didn't seem to be upset about the fact the information was in the hands of the public. He told the judge, "The technology was best placed in the hands of the people rather than the military industrial complex." He said, "While I don't condone what the two defendants did, I am a futurist at heart, and I see a world in front of us where so much can be changed. Never before has our planet been so close to equality and sustainability." Lax and Lad were surprised by Chambers' speech. They had both assumed they had ruined someone's career when they leaked the information, but the opposite looked to be true. Chambers landed on his feet and might have even been thriving. When Alex and Chris discussed their time in court over the phone in their first call after the trial, Alex pointed out that Chambers' knowledge and expertise was likely never more important.

Other speakers shared opinions with the judge. There was a hawkish military type who demanded Lax and Lad face the maximum allowable sentence and said, "Our nation can survive these fools, but we cannot allow their treason to be taken lightly." There was a libertarian senator who said all information gained by the government should be public property. There were Sanderson supporting climate activists who extolled the climate virtues of the new technology. Hyperbole was thick in the room as the activists said Winking was the only way to save humanity from pending climate cataclysms. There were business representatives arguing both sides. Transportation companies were staunchly against the tech while hotel chains were in support. Manufacturers, tech companies, even medical companies spoke about how their industries could be transformed. It was a referendum on the political future of the tech. The court of public opinion was playing out in the court and it seemed to Lax and Lad that the pro-Winking crowd had clearly won the debate, until a woman took her turn to speak.

The woman's name was Maritza Lopez. She was young, meek and had a modest beauty that was accentuated by her obvious pain. She slumped as she recounted the story of how her life was wrecked by Winking. "My husband was a writer for the Associated Press in our home country of Venezuela. He was a good man, a wonderful husband, and..." Maritza's voice broke, tears welled in her eyes and she bowed her head to hide her emotion though her feelings were obvious to everyone listening, "father to our beautiful son."

Maritza steeled herself and started talking quickly, as if the words had to rush out or else be trapped within her forever. "He told the truth about the politicians in our country and made many powerful enemies. We barely escaped a state police raid on our home when we made our way to the United States as political refugees. We were safe here. We were supposed to be safe here!" Maritza's voice pitched higher as her frustration and anger came through in her words. "My husband continued to print the truth of our country from our home here in the United States, even after we received death threats telling us to stop making trouble and calling us traitors. We believed we were safe, and so he kept writing. Last month, the three of us were having dinner. I had to use the restroom and went upstairs. I heard rustling downstairs, and I thought it was just my husband and son playing around. When I got down stairs...when I found my husband...and when I found my son, they had been stabbed and the front door was open. On the doorstep was a Wink pad that was delivered in a UPS package. The murderers managed to just mail us a Wink unit and have it set outside of our front door, break in, kill my husband and baby boy, and Wink back to Venezuela before I could make it back from the bathroom. Nowhere is safe anymore. Nowhere will ever be safe again because of the plague these two released. They haven't saved the world. They have cost me everything." Now sobbing, Maritza sat down and quietly wept as a woman sitting next to her patted her back and whispered to her.

Chris was miserable that night. He called Alex, but Alex didn't answer. Mrs. Lopez's story was so profound, it had drowned out all the other positives that had come up that day. Chris knew that the good stories would only come with tech being legal. Until then it was mostly bad. He knew he didn't cause the death of Mr. Lopez and their little boy directly, but the weight of it sat on him. In a sad attempt to wash off the day, Chris took a shower when he got home. He sat under the water until it ran cold and cried.

The next day, Alex and Chris stood before the judge to hear their sentence. They weren't worried about a surprise because the plea agreement had already been approved by the judge, but both were apprehensive about being admonished by the judge in light of Maritza Lopez's testimony. While Lax and Lad stood, on stage in the room, feeling naked, the judge said, "After hearing from both support witnesses and potential victims and in honor of the plea agreement presented by the prosecution, it is the decision of this court that the defendants will be remanded to federal prison for no less than 6 months. The defendants shall report to custody in 3 days and will stay on house arrest until that time. It is clear to this court that the impact of the leaked information has yet to be determined. While there is great promise in the technology, there has been, and there will likely continue to be harm. I hope the defendants recognize the gravity of their actions and continue to put their efforts into making amends by advocating for the good of the technology and working toward a brighter future."

Going home after the hearing was a relief to Chris and Alex and knowing they would find themselves in the same prison made the prospect of being locked up much more tolerable, just like riding home together after the hearing helped Chris cope with everything he had heard that day. Alex's father drove, his mother was in the passenger seat and the Stevens' caravanned behind. Alex and Chris didn't talk much on the ride other than to plan a conversation that night. They had become accustomed to keeping their business between the two of them and having the Chens in the car felt like being in public. So, Lax and Lad mostly looked out their windows, hugged by their seatbelts, and contemplated what the coming months would look like. Alex thought about what it might be like to go to prison, not out of worry but with the detached curiosity of a documentarian. What would the beds be like, would they delouse him like in the movies, strip search him, and give him prison-issued underwear? How would it feel to go to the bathroom in his cell with his cellmate, even if it was Chris, looking on? And of course, the showers. Alex decided he'd seen too many movies and TV shows.

Chris, on the other hand, was trapped in thoughts of the farther future. What would it be like when they were out? Would the Wink tech be ubiquitous? Would they be able to pop to the beach in Fiji? If they could, so could everyone else. All the beaches would be crowded or maybe it would be the forests or the big cities where everyone would flock. A world without boundaries. Wouldn't that mean a world without borders, without laws, a world of pure anarchy?

The Chens pulled up to the Stevens' house, let Chris out and drove home. Alex and his father exchanged only a few words on the drive. Mr. Chen told Alex he was glad everything was settled and he couldn't wait for Alex to be home. Mr. Chen admitted to missing Alex and said Mrs. Chen had some rough nights while they were in Mongolia. Alex said he was glad it was almost over too and said things would be different when he came home from prison. Mr. Chen reminded Alex of his commitments to Senator Sanderson which effectively ended their conversation in the car and in large part all their conversations before Alex left for prison.

Lax and Lad spoke that evening and agreed on the plans for the next few days. They would do a press conference the next day, an interview with Senator Sanderson the day after that, and try to relax on the third. Alex asked, "What are you going to do after the Sanderson interview? I don't really have anything planned. My dad and I aren't really talking, Amy has practice, and when my mom and I talk, she sort of just gets teary and quiet now."

"I'm not really sure. Probably leave some messages in chat channels, record a quick video for Silverberg and the guys at Zorak. I sort of promised them one last bump. I know it sounds odd, but I was thinking a long bath might be a good idea. Just some quiet. I don't think I'll get that for a while." Chris answered.

"Good call. Do you think we'll be in the same cell?" Alex asked, showing some exceedingly rare signs of worry.

"I hope so dude, but who knows? Either way it shouldn't be for long, right? Sanderson is going to get us out." Chris used his best reassuring tone.

"Man, I hope he gets elected," said Alex.

"Me too dude...me too."

***

"Okay guys, do you have your talking points? Are you both comfortable?" The Sanderson handler was clearly concerned that Lax and Lad might go off script even though they had done a few runs through the prepared talking points and every time the handler seemed happy with the outcome. What the handler didn't realize was how eager they were to get the interview right and curry the favor of what they hoped would soon be the next president. It meant three months less time in prison; not many motivations in life are as clear.

"Got the notes, and I am feeling good." Chris said.

"All good here." Alex answered from his end of the video feed. The crew had set up cameras and telelink in each of Alex and Chris' living rooms. It was surprising how much more equipment the television crew needed compared to the super low-tech interviews the two had done in their "warren" in Mongolia.

The talking points were easy. Talk up the benefits of Winking. Tie it to climate, medicine, and NASA's trips to the moon, an area Sanderson had started talking about lately. Sanderson was calling for another Kennedy-esque moon shot, but this time they would launch a remote operated rover carrying a Wink unit to the planet. The rover would deploy a prefabricated origami moon base with a built in Wink unit, and the team would just Wink an astronaut with resources to the moon. It would kick off moon colonization in earnest. Sanderson said it needed to be quick; right when he took office. After all, the Chinese and Russians had access to the Wink tech since it was leaked, and they were already on their way to stake a claim. Alex and Chris needed to emphasize that Sanderson was the only candidate with the drive and policy agenda that could take full advantage of the Wink tech.

"Great to hear. We go live in 3 minutes. Good luck and remember, you are on with the next president of the United States. It's a big deal. Treat it with respect." The handler said and then went off camera. Sanderson appeared with his gray hair and face that was somehow thin and thick at the same time. He was neither fat nor thin but had the look of someone who knew what it was like to be fat and had worked hard to try and keep the pounds off. He had longer white sideburns, a relic of his youth no doubt, and a smile that went on for days. It was infectious. Alex and Chris couldn't wait to hear him talk. Sanderson was sure to get a few signature folksy sayings during this interview. Did he plan them or were they spontaneous? Chris resolved to ask one day, if he got another chance.

"Alrighty, you boys ready for the show?" Sanderson asked jovially.

"For sure, and thanks for everything you're doing for us. We talked it out, we would have supported you either way." Chris said, without a hint of insincerity.

"Thanks for that. Means a lot to me. You boys really do have the vision and now you have a public forum. Don't waste it, and you'll make a difference for millions of people. You'll have a legacy." Sanderson responded and true to form he added, "It's not like you could support the other guy anyway. You're both smart, and he doesn't know whether to check his ass or scratch his watch." That set both Alex and Chris at ease. This interview might be fun. "Here we go," were the final words Sanderson said, and they were counted into the live feed.

"Hello America! I am joined today by two people who are often in the news these days, Alex Chen and Chris Stevens. They have had a lot of adventures recently and are about to embark on another as they head off to meet the consequences of leaking the Winking Technology. Now, I know not everyone can see what they did as patriotic, but I would bet dollars to doughnuts that in a few years everyone will understand the incredible impact this new technology will have on our world. We have a real opportunity, in the right hands of course, to change our relationship with our planet, with outer space, and with each other. Our administration intends to bring Winking to the world, make it safe for all to use, and seize this opportunity for America and Americans. The tech was created by our best and brightest and we should reap the rewards that go along with our ingenuity.

"I know a presidential candidate isn't supposed to appear with two convicted felons. And I certainly know it's unseemly to ask a couple of jailbirds to support my campaign. This is different, and I am sure you will all see why when these boys talk. You'll see their good intentions. You'll see what I saw. These boys see the future, and you'll want to be part of it too, even the skeptical folks from my stretch of the woods where people still call sushi 'bait.'

"So, without any further ado, may I introduce Chris and Alex. Say hello boys." Sanderson was still all smiles as the watching world turned their gaze on Alex and Chris.

"Thank you, Senator Sanderson. Alex and I are committed to making sure the world sees and realizes the promise of the Wink technology. When we first released the designs for the Wink tech, Alex and I were concerned with how it was being used. Winking was relegated to illegal activity but it is so much more than that. It's a transformational technology no less important than the first cars or airplanes. We have to find a way to use Winking to improve our world. Cars and planes can be used to do bad things, but on balance, they have done so much good for the world that we accept their risks. Winking is the same. The technology can't be limited because of a few bad users. Senator Sanderson is right! It's our tech. Let's make it our own and show the world all the good that can be done. We can save lives, save the planet, and explore in ways we never thought would be possible." Chris was on a roll. They weren't supposed to talk long. Alex secretly thought it was because the handlers were afraid of what might be said if Lax and Lad were allowed to go on too long. "Imagine a day where you can Wink to the office. No commute. No traffic. No frustration. Want to go on vacation to Hawaii? Wink and you're there. Want to bounce on the moon? Just Wink to Selenean Summit. Your life will be better, and Senator Sanderson is the only person running for president who is trying to make that happen. He had our vote from the moment we first talked to him."

Senator Sanderson cut in as Chris was taking a breath to speak again. He apparently felt they were on a high note and wanted to close the conversation. Timing is everything in politics, and Sanderson had the timing nailed. "That is wonderful to hear Chris. I surely do appreciate your support, and I agree, it's time to take our fate in our hands. We are Americans and we can do anything. Let's move forward together, America." 'Forward Together' was Sanderson's campaign slogan and he worked it into his speech like working a hand into a well-worn glove. Chris didn't speak at the press conference again, and Alex managed to avoid speaking at all according to his preference. Sanderson was far from done. He spoke for another 20 minutes recapping his platform of liberal reforms, always mixing his brand of humor with sharp words for the current administration and emphasizing how optimistic he was for the changes his administration would bring. If he was able to accomplish half of what he was promising, Alex thought while they listened, it would be pretty amazing.

After the press conference, Alex called Chris for the last time before they would be imprisoned. The moment had come but neither of the hackers were truly ready. Their Mongolian hotel experience was somehow not enough to help them feel prepared on the eve of their true incarceration, regardless of what they thought or said in their late-night conversations.

Alex said to Chris, "Looking forward to hanging out with you in the yard. Should we pick the biggest guy and start a fight?"

Chris smiled; Alex's dry humor was a safety blanket but it worked. "How about we just hide in a corner as much as possible until Sanderson gets us out. Maybe we can pull an Andy Duphrane and make ourselves useful to the warden."

"I don't know how to do taxes though. We could try the tech support angle. I'm sure the warden needs a couple computer guys." Alex picked up the thread, the way he always did. Lax and Lad laughed. At least they had each other. They would make it through prison just like they made it through everything else, together.

Lax and Lad (4)

Sojourn

Otisville Federal Penitentiary is home to politicians, bankers, and a variety of other white collar elite criminals. Forbes ranked it as a "cushy" prison. Lax and Lad landed in the cushy prison because of Chris's diligence and once they had arrived, Alex was rightly appreciative. The guards who oriented the two on the first day made a point of telling them how lucky they were to be in the same prison. That was not normal. According to the guard, they "must have friends in high places." Alex and Chris knew that it was likely Senator Sanderson being a friend again. Clearly their decision to support Sanderson was one of the best decisions they had made.

The prison was surprisingly small and more comfortable than their self-imposed jail in Mongolia. There were only 120 inmates who milled about the property in what seemed like relative leisure. There was to be a disproportionate number of gray-haired, overweight inmates which added to a sense of safety for Alex and Chris. There was a library, a television viewing room, and a gym. Things in the prison were old but serviceable. To Alex, it bore a surprising resemblance to the prison in "Orange is the New Black," minus the ladies and the porn-stache.

The sleeping areas at the prison were ringed around a central common area that felt more like a college quad than a prison. On the other end of the quad was a prison kitchen and leisure facilities. There weren't any cells. The prison was set up more like an army barracks with large open rooms filled with bunk beds and guards patrolling at all hours.

The first day at Otisville was orientation for Lax and Lad. They received their uniforms, were pleased to find they would be sharing a bunk bed together, and got a general lay of the land. While not all of their worries were assuaged, it seemed livable. They found out they would be working outside since they were part of the Otisville prison camp. They would be assigned to the grounds crew where they would help maintain the grounds of the Otisville camp and the attached medium security prison.

The first night was difficult for Chris in particular. The wide-open room felt vulnerable, even with Alex in the bunk below him, especially compared to the claustrophobia of the hotel room in Mongolia. Chris felt exposed. Alex, on the other hand, seemed to sleep like a baby. When they woke up for their first morning, Alex was refreshed, not cheery, but not nearly as sullen as he seemed the days leading up to their incarceration.

"You seem to be holding up okay." Chris said to Alex when he hopped off his bunk.

"Yeah, this feels like the downhill part. There's an end in sight. You know what I mean?" Alex said while stretching his arms and surveying the room. There were men everywhere. It was noisy because the walls and floors were concrete and the din of everyone talking was bouncing around like a resonating chamber.

"Makes sense. I slept like shit. It just feels like someone's staring at me in the dark." It was nice to have Alex there to admit this to. What would Chris have done if they were separated?

"Dude, they are. The guards are watching all the time," quipped Alex.

"Fair point. Do we go for food now?" Asked Alex.

"Looks like it." Chris pointed to a queue of guys at the door out to the quad.

"Do you suppose they have any of that awesome curdled milk?" Alex smiled. Chris chuckled in return and they made their way into the queue.

The queue turned out to be for the bathroom and showers. The men in line were getting ready to head out to work for the day. Chris and Alex weren't assigned to duty on their first day and were happy to avoid the showers and go back to their bunks to sit down as the common area cleared out. It was an odd experience as neither really understood what they were meant to do and there were no guards stepping up to lead them. There were a few other prisoners milling around but Lax and Lad decided to keep to themselves.

After 30 minutes of chatting, Chris told Alex he was going to check with a guard. He stood up and walked to a guard standing near the exit door. Alex watched the exchange. From his vantage point, it looked like Chris talked for about 10 seconds, the guard seemed to give no reply, and Chris scurried back over to their bunk. "What happened?" Alex asked as Chris approached.

"That was enlightening. I don't think he even looked at me. He said talk to an 'old-timer.'" Chris shrugged his shoulders and waived his hands signaling the entirety of the bunk area. Alex followed Chris's hand and looked for a friendly face. Chris said, "Well, at least we didn't do anything wrong. I can't imagine the guard just letting it go."

"Guess not. What about that guy over there? He looks pretty harmless." Alex pointed at a guy staring down at a book lying in the lower bed of a bunk three rows over. They walked over together hoping the decision was the right one.

The man on the bed had long gray hair pulled into a ponytail and had just flipped to his stomach to continue his reading. He was thick, leaning towards fat, but it was clear there was a big layer of muscle under his bulk. Still his face was kind. A smile seemed to be on his face by default and he looked vaguely hippyish with longer white sideburns and a soul patch under his bottom lip. The man had noticed the two coming over, never looking up from his book he said, "You lost?"

"The guard said we should ask someone else and we were kinda hoping you could tell us...what are we supposed to be doing?" Chris asked nervously, knowing he sounded like a child.

The man laughed heartily and said, "Figures. First day, huh?"

"Yeah," Chris replied.

"Okay then, here's the deal." He closed his book around his pointer finger to keep his place, rolled over and sat up to look them in the eyes. "This place is on a schedule, but it's pretty relaxed if you don't have work. I hurt my knee and got a med pass for a few days." He tapped at his right knee and smiled. "It's your first day, so no work for you, but expect something tomorrow. Then you get up, hit the showers, hit the head and follow the crowd. There's a foreman and he'll tell you what to do. Today, get the lay of the land. You really just need to be at your bunk for roll call and in the mess for chow. Chow's at eleven and roll is at one. After roll, you get some free time again. There's plenty of shit to do. Take my advice and avoid crowded areas. The library's a good place to be or maybe check out the handball courts outside. Either way, keep your eyes open and your mouths shut until you have things figured out. If someone tells you to do something...do it. You get too lost, go talk to the chaplain or that guard over there." He pointed across the barracks to a guard who was smiling and talking to a skinny, twitchy younger inmate. "The rest could give two shits." He lifted his book and said, "Good enough?"

Chris was sensitive about asking too much from this guy. He said thank you as earnestly as he could and he and Alex made their way back to their bunks, their homebase.

"Let's explore then. I need to go to the bathroom. Can we go there first?" Chris asked Alex, who just nodded. Sweet relief. In the bathroom, the toilets had stalls and so did the showers. They weren't the communal showers they always showed in the movies. They looked like bathroom stalls with tan walls and a door that closed and latched. There was a man just finishing a shower. They noticed he took the towel into the shower with him and noted that as protocol for the next day. After the bathroom they made their way across the quad. They sat in the television room for a little bit, walked through the library and hit the gold mine when they made it to the computer room. It was clear the computers were not state of the art. Most still had tube monitors from the 90s and a bunch were out of commission, but there were at least a few that had a browser open. They could get to email. They could at least keep up with the outside world. Another reason to relax, following two stressful days of anticipation quickly followed by welcomed surprises.

They made their way back to bunk for roll and noticed the quantity of other inmates and how packed in they all were. The feeling of sleeping in the wide open was replaced with a new feeling of claustrophobia. The goal after roll would be to make at least one friend. It turned out to be easier than they thought. The skinny, twitchy kid they had seen talking to the nice guard earlier came over and talked to them.

"Hey, ain't you those two hackers who did the Wink tech thing? I saw you on TV the other day," he said before he even got to Lax and Lad. His voice was louder than either would have preferred. "Man, there's famous people all over this place. That dude over there is an ex-senator. That one was some famous banker guy who stole millions of dollars from his customers. Long as I keep up on my TV, I can spot 'em a mile away. My name's Ricky, but they call me Ratty around here." He reached out his hand to Alex. It was a painfully awkward moment as Alex clearly paused to consider if shaking Ratty's hand was a good idea. Alex relented and shook the hand and Chris did next. Chris noticed a guy one bunk over watching them closely and another small group looking their way periodically. He wasn't sure if being a celebrity would be a good thing or a bad thing in prison. Time would tell. In the meantime, having a friend would be nice. Ratty was as good as any. His nickname was right on the mark. He had medium-length, greasy, dark hair that looked like it could use a wash. He was exceedingly thin with prominent cheekbones and a long nose. In short, he looked a little like a wet rat.

"You are those guys, right?" Ratty asked again.

"That's us," said Chris.

"Well, I haven't winked or nothin' yet but it sounds cool as hell. You guys are good at computers, right?" Ratty asked eagerly.

"Yeah, pretty good I guess." Chris replied.

"Sweeet. We need someone good with computers 'round here. A ton of the ones in the lab aren't working, the guards don't know how to fix 'em and it's not like the prison is going to pay someone to come in and fix 'em." Ratty seemed excited at the prospect of getting access. Chris guessed that, given Ratty's size, when the computers didn't work, he wasn't likely to get priority over the bigger inmates.

"We noticed earlier. We'll take a look." Alex weighed in.

"Sweeeet!" said Ratty.

Alex and Chris thought they just found their Shawshank skill that would help them with their time in the prison. It was good to be needed. They would have something to focus their attention on and hopefully help inmates in the process, which would keep them safe.

Alex asked, "Are we supposed to be places other than chow and line up? We haven't really figured that out yet."

"No one really expects much day one but you'll find the groove tomorrow. You'll go off to work the yard and then sort of follow the herd. It'll make sense pretty quick." Ratty answered somewhat distractedly. He was looking around the room like he had accomplished his goal and was now looking for somewhere better to be.

"Cool. Any advice for tomorrow then? Like do we need to be somewhere or avoid someone?" Chris asked anxiously, probing for information.

"Show up at 7:00 out front for work. Shower and clean up before you go. Pisses off people on the crews if you smell bad. If you end up doing yard at the medium-security facility, watch your back. Those guys aren't as laid back as us." Ratty added, "Hey see you guys around. I need to head over there." He pointed to a pack of other fidgety people in a circle a few yards from where they were.

"Cool, See you around." Chris said.

When Ratty departed Alex and Chris sat and talked about the next day. After work they would head over to the computer lab and see about fixing anything they could. Chris said the sooner the better. They wanted to be in as many good graces as they could, even though nothing they had seen seemed terribly dangerous to either of them. Better safe than sorry.

The next morning Chris woke up at 6:30, roused Alex and they followed Ratty's advice. They made their way to the showers, cleaned up and lined up for work duty. A guard counted them in for duty and gave them a nod as if to say, "Glad you figured it out on your own. I thought you were going to make more work for me by not being where you needed to be." They were going to the medium security facility for yard work that day. The inmates were packed on buses and driven for only a minute or so. Alex thought it was silly, they could have walked the distance faster since they had to load up, count, unload, count again and then walk to their work areas.

Lax and Lad ended up with a truly crappy job. They were assigned to clean the pigeon droppings from all the walkways in the medium-security yard. They had to wear masks as they cleaned since the bird dropping was toxic in quantity. To clean the concrete, they used scrub brushes. Most of the work was done with scrub brushes that looked like large brooms but they had small brushes for getting the caked-on hard to clear spots. For those spots, they would have to get down on their hands and knees and really scrub.

The walkway went around the whole yard in a big dog-leg shape, passing the building for a decent stretch. The section of walkway closest to the building was by far the most caked with bird droppings but the most unpleasant part of the cleaning experience occurred near the baseball diamond situated in the northeast corner of the grounds. It wasn't the bird droppings that made the section unpleasant, though there were plenty of droppings to worry about. No, it was the proximity to a large group of medium-security inmates. It was colder outside but the diamond was being used by a relatively sizable group of inmates playing softball with no gloves and another group watching and periodically shouting obscenities at the players. As Alex and Chris approached with their broom-scrubbers, the inmates started harassing them.

The first to engage were the inmates on the bench. They started with cat calls, shouting things like, "Fresh meat," and "Look, new maids. Hey, can one of you come fluff my pillow." Alex and Chris just kept their heads down and scrubbed. Things escalated when the game actually stopped as they scrubbed the area behind home plate. It turned into a group activity, and all the inmates joined in. A group was in front and another was behind them as they went, all talking, but not shouting to avoid too much attention from the guards. Alex and Chris both looked around for the guards to see when someone would come help. They saw a pair of guards standing near the building entrance about 50 yards away, but they seemed too wrapped in conversation to care about what was happening with Alex and Chris.

"Alex, let's just keep scrubbing. We'll be past these guys soon." Chris said, turning his head to Alex on his right. Alex's head was down and he was scrubbing hard with the broom. He looked worried. Chris was worried too and became even more worried when he saw one of the inmates standing, not shouting right next to Alex with his hands in his pockets. The inmate's posture looked wrong; his face looked wrong. There was something about his presence that said he was preparing. Chris stood up all the way just in time to see the inmate pull his hands out of his pockets and rush at Alex. There was a thud and the inmate was on top of Alex. Alex yelled, "What the hell!!" and Chris watched Alex lean over from the weight of the attacking inmate. The attacker had his left shoulder under Alex and his head resting on Alex's back. The inmate's right arm shifted back and forth under Alex, hidden from view, as if he was punching Alex in the stomach, but something was still off. The noises coming from Alex weren't the sounds of gut punches. The rest of the inmates were backing away. The guards were starting to run over, and Chris finally acted. He jumped on the attacking inmate, who quickly turned his attention to Chris. The two ended up tied up like two boxers late in a match. Chris had his arms around the inmate's midsection and the inmate had his arms over Chris' shoulders. Chris was pushing the attacker back and felt punches on his back. Only the punches didn't feel right. They felt sharper, narrower. Chris shoved the inmate off and saw something glinting in his hand. A toothbrush? The handle was sharp. Chris felt faint, his breathing felt hard and he had foam in his mouth. The world went dark just as Chris saw the guards tackle the attacking inmate.

***

Chris woke up in a hospital bed. For a while, he just listened to the sounds of the hospital, mind blank. He heard shuffling feet, the beeping and whirring from medical equipment, doors opening and closing and a television on in another room. When thought came back to Chris it came slowly. He remembered being in prison, scrubbing concrete with Alex and a fight. It all felt surreal and distant but Chris knew it was real. He hurt. There was stabbing pain deep in his chest every time he took a deep breath and his back was achy and tender. A toothbrush had done so much damage. He wondered if Alex was already awake and a room or two away or was Alex already back at Otisville having to make his way on his own. Maybe it was Alex's TV in the other room. Chris hit the red call button on the side of the hospital bed to bring in the nurse who arrived within a few minutes.

"Good to see you awake, how long have you been up?" asked the nurse as she checked Chris's various plugs and wires. She removed the tape that was over his I.V. which caused the area to itch.

"Only for a few minutes," Chris said, unsure about the protocol for prisoners waking up in a hospital. Were there guards outside waiting for him? "Is it okay for me to ask you a few questions?"

"I can try to give you some good answers, but you might want to ask your dad. He's here somewhere. Probably just ran down to get some more coffee." The nurse walked over to the side of Chris's bed and pressed the button to lift it into an upright position. Chris shifted as the bed leaned forward. The movements were painful and incredibly stiff.

"My dad's here?" It was a welcome surprise for Chris. "How long was I out?"

"Let's see," the nurse grabbed the chart attached to the foot of the bed. "You've been here for ten days. It looks like you've woken up a couple times before but were listed as 'minimally conscious.' So, you may not remember."

For the rest of the information, the nurse suggested talking to the doctor or to Mr. Stevens. The limited conversation left Chris exhausted and he dozed off. He woke up a few hours later, and this time his father was sitting at the edge of the bed in the chair that was stationed in the hospital room. Seeing the chair, Chris noted that the chair resembled the chair in the hotel room in Mongolia. It was made of a light wood with the same wooden low back covered by durable fabric that looked as though it had been well used. His dad was at the edge of the chair with his elbows resting on the bed. Chris realized he must have shown signs of waking up, maybe muttering or shifting in the bed, since he couldn't imagine his dad sitting in that leaned over position for long. Chris mumbled, "Hey, Dad." His voice was still weak and he didn't have enough energy to look around and talk. He closed his eyes as he said, "How are things?"

Mr. Stevens chuckled at the question since it was clearly too narrow considering the gravity of everything that happened in the previous couple of weeks…months…years. He said, "They've been better. How are you feeling?"

"I'm sore." Chris shuffled in the bed. "And really exhausted. What the hell happened? I remember the fight but I can't really make much sense out of the events in my head."

"Well…" Mr. Stevens paused, clearly considering what he should say first. "You were stabbed 6 times in the back with a makeshift weapon made out of a toothbrush. Do you remember that?" Chris nodded and Mr. Stevens continued. "You passed out at the prison. You weren't getting much oxygen because you were stabbed in the lungs and you were losing a lot of blood. The guards called in your injury really quickly and were able to keep you somewhat stable while the medical staff came over. It was actually pretty lucky you were stabbed where you were. The medical staff are all housed at the medium-security facility, and you weren't far from the Health Services office. They called in EMT support who rushed you to this hospital where they performed emergency surgery to repair and close the wounds. You've been out the whole time. We were starting to worry about you not waking up." Tears welled up in Mr. Stevens eyes at the thought and his voice broke as he continued. "Your mother and I have been taking turns to be with you every day. I called her, and she's on her way. Just a warning…she's going to be a crying mess when she gets here."

Eyes still closed, Chris smiled. "So, who was that guy who stabbed us and is Alex in the room next door or did he already go back?"

"The guy was waiting for you. His name was Timothy McNally. After he stabbed you and the guards came over, he tried to use the toothbrush to stab a guard. The guard shoved him away and he landed with the toothbrush through his eye. He didn't make it." Mr. Stevens paused, expecting a question.

Chris obliged, "Holy shit. Why was he waiting for us? I've never heard of him."

"Mr. McNally had a brother in the military. His brother was a green beret. Apparently, they had a tip about a terrorist target in a building outside of Kabul. They went to raid the building, but when they got in there, they couldn't find any people. They did find a room full of wink units and a camera. When they entered the room, a dozen men Winked in with guns and killed the Marines. The tip about the location was a decoy to get the Marines in that room. McNally blamed you and Alex for letting the tech get into the hands of the terrorist. He saw you were going to be sent to Otisville in the news and was waiting for a chance to get to you. He got that chance early. He was in the yard near the softball field and saw you coming." Mr. Stevens broke off and waited again for the next question.

Chris waited in silence for a few minutes. It was almost too much to take in. When he eventually spoke again, he asked, "Where's Alex then? He shouldn't be back at that prison. It's dangerous."

"Chris…Alex…didn't make it. McNally stabbed him in the heart and he was gone by the time the medical staff was able to help him." Mr. Stevens's tears started to flow in earnest. He saw the shock and pain on his son's face and he felt the pain twofold. Once for his own loss of Alex, as his son's best friend and a near member of the family over the years. The other for his son's loss. Seeing the pain on Chris's face made him remember his son as a child and his wish, the same wish every father has, that he could prevent his son from feeling the pain of the world. He reached over and grabbed Chris's hand, placed it between his two hands and leaned his head down until Chris's hand was completely covered with his hands and forehead and the two wept together until Chris fell asleep again.

Chris slept for ten hours after the hard news. He woke to his mother at his side. They cried together as he did with his father. Mrs. Stevens did her best to console him, but there was really nothing she could say that would ease Chris's suffering. She knew the most a mother can do is be there and share in the pain. She told him that time would heal his hurt and that Alex would want him to find a way forward, a way to do good. She told him that he had a long life ahead of him and there were so many beautiful things to see and new relationships that will help fill the hole he felt. The words were not empty. Mrs. Stevens believed them but she knew that they were all just words this early in the loss. After their time together, Mrs. Stevens found her way to the cafeteria, had a coffee, and hung her head to cry on her own. Chris slept for another twelve hours.

Over the following days, Chris came to grips with his new reality, though he still hurt. His parents were always at his side. Alex's parents and Amy, Alex's sister, came to see him in the hospital as well. They brought magazines and Alex's favorite books, the Ender's Game saga. The Chen's thanked Chris for jumping in to help Alex. Mr. Chen said to Chris, "Showed how strong your friendship with Alex was. You were brothers and that makes you part of this family. If you ever need anything, we are here." Chris's heart broke again.

The doctors told Chris he would be in the hospital for a few months to recover and that he would require physical therapy to get back on his feet. Chris was secretly relieved he wouldn't have to go back to the prison right away. He knew the prison would present another set of emotional challenges. He would be alone in a place that he thought was safe but was actually mortally dangerous. The only person he knew there was Ratty and somehow that seemed woefully inadequate. Senator Sanderson had yet to call, but Chris was watching the news and Sanderson seemed sure to win the presidency. He had attempted to curry favor with the liberals with his pitch to improve the environment using Wink tech. The conservatives were voting based on his goals for American exceptionalism. America would be the first to colonize the moon, beating out the Chinese, Russians, Europeans and Japanese. Sanderson also promised America would lead the Wink tech sales boom that was sure to come once the tech was no longer illegal. If Chris was lucky, he would never have to go back to Otisville.

The elections were held a month after Chris woke up in the hospital. The polls showed a ten-point lead for Sanderson and after the votes were tallied Sanderson ended up with a twelve-point victory. A landslide election that hadn't been seen since Reagan's win over Carter in 1980. Sanderson had a clear mandate from the people to get Wink tech out to the world and to make it safe.

A couple weeks after the election Chris received a call from Sanderson. Sanderson was compassionate and caring. He seemed to truly feel Alex's loss and to sympathize with Chris. He told Chris he wouldn't let him go back to jail and that he would speak publicly about their shared loss of Alex and then announce Chris's pardon. The pardon would be among the first things he would do once in office. Chris thanked Sanderson and felt at ease and alone.

True to his word, President Elect Sanderson held a press conference a few days later. The Stevens' watched together in Chris's hospital room. Sanderson said, "We look forward to a world, to an America, made more fruitful, livable and exciting because of the Wink tech. Winking will redefine our relationship to home, to work, to each other, to the world and to our solar system. It will be a transformation the likes of which has been unparalleled in human history. Flight, space-travel, the moon landing, and the internet will hardly register compared to the scale of change brought about by the Wink tech, and the world sorely needs change. We can do better and we will do better. We wouldn't be able to make these steps forward without the brave actions of two young men, Alex Chen and Chris Stevens, who took it upon themselves to share the tech with the world.

"As many of you likely already know, Alex and Chris came back to America and turned themselves in and were sent to prison as penance for their acts, but tragedy struck and Alex was stabbed to death in jail." Sanderson paused, collecting himself. "I had the honor of knowing Alex. He was young and full of promise. He was bright and eager to help the world. If he's not in a better place, the rest of us don't stand a chance." Another long pause. "I want to renew my commitment to Chris Stevens, who now sits in a hospital recovering from his own stab wounds but without his best friend who he tried to save from their attacker. I will not allow Chris to go back to prison. As one of my first acts in office, I will pardon Chris and ask him to consult with my administration on how best to bring Wink tech to the world."

Sanderson went on to talk about other policies and appointments, but Chris muted the TV. He was touched by Sanderson's words though Chris thought Sanderson may have overplayed his relationship with Alex. Alex was mostly quiet when they spoke. It was a play for sympathy that was meant to ingratiate Sanderson to the public, but it had the added benefits of honoring Alex and freeing Chris. Also, would Chris actually get to work with the administration? Sanderson hadn't mentioned it to him in their call. When he gave it some thought, Chris was excited to help guide the future of the Wink tech. Before Sanderson mentioned Chris's consultation with the new administration, Chris was feeling lost and devoid of purpose. Now, purpose was right in front of him and he had hope again.

Lad (5)

Sage Mode

College life had changed significantly by the time Chris Stevens had taken his post at the Hawaii Institute of Technology, HIT for short. Lots of things had changed. Wink tech started the world down a whole new path. Chris, having been part of the Lax and Lad team that was the catalyst, had become a minor celebrity which made him an excellent candidate for government agencies and university teaching posts. HIT offered Chris a professorship in techno-ethics and quarters near campus, though where you lived was really up to you and the resources you had at your disposal since the commute from anywhere on the planet was nearly instantaneous. Hawaii was sought after by the affluent around the world for its beauty and excellent weather. Securing a place to live on a Hawaiian island was difficult since anyone could Wink to work anywhere on the planet and Wink back home at the end of the day. There were no barriers, no island fever, no need for really expensive food on the island, no need for Spam to be a staple, though it still was. Winking had flattened the Earth. Transporting goods or people was near instantaneous. You could get a pizza delivered from Chicago in the same time it took you to get one from the local pizza joint.

The new flat Earth meant that desirable places to live became much more desirable and the bottom dropped out in places where living was hard. The map of the planet shifted. When the living was harsh, people avoided living there, but it didn't prevent businesses from flourishing. Businesses owned skyscrapers and sprawling office complexes in the strangest places, where the land was cheap and easy to build on. HIT was built on Hawaii's big island to attract students from around the world. The real estate came as a land grant. It would have been impossible to afford to build otherwise.

Chris's classroom looked much like college lecture halls had looked through the decades. The room had stadium seating that curved out in front of a desk with a sizable smart presentation board behind it that allowed Chris to present, write notes, and call up anything that could be searched on the internet via voice command. While the tech wasn't that new, having it in college classrooms was the purview of the wealthy schools, which included HIT. The differences between Chris's class and classes in the pre-Wink world were the students. Anyone from anywhere on the planet could attend provided they met the basic criteria: they could pay the ridiculously high tuition which had increased dramatically since college students were able to cut out the cost of campus housing in favor of staying home and Winking to class, they met the admissions criteria which required near perfection since the competition for entry became global, and they could show enough English proficiency to participate in the class when called upon. English proficiency was barely an issue anymore. English was already the language of business before Wink tech became globally ubiquitous, now everyone on the planet learned English as a primary language in school.

The Earth was almost completely flat. So flat that schools realized they could specialize in a specific subject since a student could Wink to Harvard for a class in law and then moments later go to Tsinghua University for an engineering class. HIT was all technology, no humanities, or general education courses. If a student wanted to take a basic English course, they could go to Oxford. There was no need for HIT to have course offerings outside of technology as long as they had reciprocity agreements with other schools around the world.

Chris's class was a rainbow of people, and he wouldn't have had it any other way. Student's perspectives were colored by nationality, family, and history, and it made for amazing conversations. Chris found he loved teaching and engaging in "big" conversations with students every day. He taught using case studies and asked his students to weigh in on the right and wrong they saw in real world scenarios which included the release of Wink tech. His direct experience made his class in high demand for students around the world. He was happy they capped the class at 200 students. The dull tasks of grading and doing study sessions were handled by his teaching assistants leaving Chris only the work he loved, or as his friend, former President Sanderson would say, "He got left with all the steak and none of the gristle."

Sanderson made good on his commitment to Chris. He pardoned Chris before Chris even made it out of the hospital. Once Chris had recovered, Sanderson had him join the administration and help guide the release of the Wink tech. They did amazing work together. One of the first moves President Sanderson made was to legalize the production of Wink units through authorized manufacturers. Sanderson's genius was in how he legalized Wink tech. He saw the impact Wink tech would have on the transportation industry, so he gave exclusive rights to two automobile manufacturers and two airlines. His smartest play was to put the four transportation companies in direct competition with Google, though with a small head start to help establish them as producers. In no time at all, Wink units were available en masse and at prices that had been driven down by competition. Of the five companies who received the initial licenses from the government, three of them became the largest companies in the country. The company's innovated safety and security features for Wink tech that prevented people from just Winking into your home without permission. It was a technology, like cell phones, that needed a constant flow of new models in the arms race against unit hacking. The tech became safer and safer and the world adopted it faster and faster. Within a few short years, Wink units replaced cars. They were much cheaper, much safer and much faster. All it took was enough units around the world to make travel anywhere possible.

All the changes Chris had worked towards with the Sanderson administration had led to the possibility of how Chris was teaching that day and it gave him a sense of satisfaction that Chris secretly thought was exceedingly rare. He was lucky. He had paid a heavy price in the early days. Losing Alex broke Chris for years. His mother was right though, time did heal Chris and he found purpose in the Wink tech. He met a girl through a dating app who was an Amsterdam native (after all he could date anyone from anywhere) and made him smile. She was reserved and smart, with a quick wit that reminded Chris of Alex. They had a son, who they named Alex. They lived in Hawaii and traveled the world in their free time.

The road to the worldwide acceptance of the Wink tech wasn't always smooth. There were bumps along the way that led to congressional hearings, protests and a fair amount of negative media. People disagreed about the value of the tech, how it was allowed to proliferate and who profited. Those disagreements were great fodder for Chris's courses and the subject of that day's conversation.

Chris sat on the edge of the center of his desk and addressed the two hundred students who were in attendance for the day's lecture. He greeted the class to settle everyone down and started in on his basic survey of the controversies that surrounded Wink tech. He covered the arguments that Wink tech made local laws unenforceable in a lot of ways and that Wink tech shut down whole industries and forced workers into unemployment. Chris described the early problems with privacy that were solved by being able to limit which Wink units could connect to your home unit. Before the improvement, anyone with your unit address could just pop into your home without asking. He also discussed the Sanderson administration's choice, under his watch, to grant distribution licenses to handpicked companies. Wasn't that anti-capitalistic? Where were the market forces? He also discussed misuses, such as burying a Wink unit underground so that when someone Winked in, they were buried alive. The conversation was dark.

"Now, we've covered the controversies and ills of Wink tech. Let me ask one question. Can technology be intrinsically good or bad?" Chris asked the class. The room was silent for a few moments as everyone waited for the first brave student to answer the question.

A young woman in the front row stood and said, "Yes. Nuclear bombs are bad and artificial hearts are good. I can't think of a good use for the bomb or a bad use for an artificial heart. The technologies have an intrinsic value."

"Ahhh! Thank you for being brave enough to jump into the deep end." Chris waved his finger in the students' direction playfully. "I would argue the opposite. It's not the technology that's bad or good. It's how it's used. The bomb as a deterrent for war could be seen as a benefit for society. It's only when the bomb is used when a value can be assigned to it. An artificial heart is only good when it is used to save someone's life. The technology on its own is neutral. We, as the human stewards of the technology, determine its value and we often don't all agree. Who can tell me what hearings are being held in front of Congress next week that would be relevant here?" Chris asked as he hopped off his desk and began to pace the front of the classroom while he looked up at the audience.

"The Wink Tech Equity hearings," came a disembodied voice from the back of the room.

"Exactly!" Chris said enthusiastically. "Next week, Congress will hear testimony in advance of legislation that would make Wink tech a public utility. The argument is that people have a fundamental right to this new means of transportation like they would a road or water running to their houses. Winking has become so ubiquitous that everyone should have access as a basic right. The car industry is basically gone as is the airline industry. The businesses are only sustainable by novelty companies for people who want to remember what it feels like to step on the gas pedal or float above the clouds, but people don't fly to get places any more. The poor need options to get to work just as much as the wealthy. City buses are nearly a thing of the past. We have come too far to turn back and restricting access to the tech through pricing or control from corporations would cause major civil issues. The debate between the capitalists and socialists is raging and both sides have interesting arguments but, at the end of the day, they aren't arguing about the tech. They are arguing about how it should be used and by whom, just like they did when cars grew in popularity or when the internet exploded. Both of which were used for amazing, great things but also horrible things. We didn't stop driving cars because people crashed or stop using the internet because it was full of trolls. The technology was the technology, we just worked our way through the challenges to find the other side, the more positive side." Chris stopped pacing, sat down and took a breath.

A student stood in the middle-left side of the class and asked, "Aren't you testifying with President Sanderson?"

"I am. Actually, he and I are meeting tonight to discuss things. He will be winking over to my house for dinner. Just another amazing use for the technology." Chris smiled at the class.

The same student asked, "What do you think you'll say?"

"I imagine the same things I just said to you," Chris replied. "The technology has reached a point that access is a public necessity. Hell, I hear there are places where people have started building houses on old, no longer used roads. The foundations were poured for them, just for a different purpose. People have started to reclaim the infrastructure. Cars can't make it from A to B anymore and what's more, the land is better used for housing than underused roads. Times have shifted, and the government needs to ensure a long life of equitable access to Wink tech. Even Though today Wink tech is cheap and access isn't limited for the average person, if the manufacture of the Wink units continues to consolidate in the hands of just a couple firms with proprietary additions to the tech, that could all change. People need to be protected from the market."

Chris's last comment sparked a long debate about free versus regulated markets and the role of the government. The students were jumping in the conversation and Chris could hear their passion. He loved it. He walked out of class after the debate feeling rejuvenated. He Winked home, kissed his wife, hugged little Alex and got ready to meet with former President Sanderson.

As Chris sat on his sofa reading to Alex, a ringing noise came from the front of the house. Chris stood, lifting Alex off his lap and setting him back down on the couch. He said aloud "accept Wink" and his unit lit up for the incoming traffic. Sanderson arrived right on time, Winking onto the pad located in the Stevens' front entryway. He stepped off the pad with a hand extended to greet Chris. The two shook hands, smiling at each other. Chris reached around Sanderson's shoulders, which were more slumped than Chris remembered, led him to the living room and offered him a drink which Sanderson declined. Chris was aware of Sanderson's age, but he didn't really register it until he saw his longtime friend and ally slouched on the couch, stature diminished, his eyes foggy and his skin liver spotted and sagging.

"So, are you ready for tomorrow?" Chris asked.

"Welp, I better be. It's an important day. In a lot of ways, it's the culmination of all of our work together. It's fitting we should go together to once again defend Wink tech." Sanderson smiled with content as if to show their work together was good work and that he was proud. "How about you? Are you up to the limelight again?"

"We had a good conversation about it in my ethics class today. I feel ready and eager. It feels a little like when Alex and I made our pitch on that hacker channel when we were still in Mongolia," said Chris.

Sanderson dropped his smile and asked, "Do you still think of Alex often?"

Chris smiled widely. "Hard not to. I did name my kid after him. An odd thing went through my head today, though. I wondered why no one in class asked me if I thought it was right of me and Alex to leak the Wink tech. More importantly, I wondered why no one has ever really asked me if it was worth it. If I'm honest, I think I wanted someone to ask."

Sanderson took his que. He fixed a smile back on his face and said, "Well, Mr. Stevens...Do you think leaking the Wink tech was right; and was it worth it?"

"The cost was high, for me, almost too high. Alex and I were close, especially after our time in Mongolia. He meant more to me than I realized. Alex was quiet, unaffected, and nearly impossible to rile up. There were times I wanted to choke him, but I loved him. Alex wasn't the only person hurt either. People did lose jobs and bad things were done with the tech that cost people their lives. Still, I love my wife and my son. Would they exist without the Wink tech? So many things in this world are better. Pollution is way down, equity and opportunity are up around the world. On balance, I think it was right, but I am still not sure it was worth it for me," Chris said. He was trying to decide the difference between what he believed and what he felt. It was clear as mud at that moment.

"That sounds right to me. Losing Alex was part of the price we paid for progress. You couldn't make chicken salad out of that chicken shit with all the mayonnaise in the world. We did what we thought was right and so did Alex, and the world is better because of it. The world owes Alex for his sacrifice and tomorrow we get to remind everyone of that." Sanderson was still a moving orator and Chris laughed at his southern charm and forgot Sanderson's age again. "After all, if what we did was wrong, then we have plenty of time to pay for it in the afterlife. We'll be okay either way. We can go to Heaven for the climate, or Hell for the company."

Chris grinned at his old friend and said, "You know when Alex and I met you all those years ago, we meant it when we said we would have gotten behind you even without the pardon. Meeting you was one of the great moments of my life." Chris leaned forward and put his hand on the backside of Sanderson's which was resting on the arm of the couch. He looked him in the eye and gave a heartfelt "Thank you for everything." He leaned back again, sighed and said, "One thing though. I have been meaning to ask you this for a long time. Those great southern sayings, where do you get them? Do you plan for them in advance? I mean...go to Hell for the company?" Chris chuckled.

"Well, that bit was Mark Twain." Sanderson said sheepishly. "The rest just comes from loving English and loving a turn of phrase. I gotta admit, in the early days, I planned a lot of them. These days though, they are as natural as breathing. What paints a better picture," Sanderson lowered his voice and dropped his southern drawl and said, "That gentleman is mentally unsound," he let his voice go back to normal, "or that guy is nuttier than a porta potty at a peanut convention?"

Chris gave a legitimate belly laugh and said, "Point taken." They sat in contented silence for a few minutes. Chris reflected on the past and broke the silence after a funny thought occurred to him. "I just realized, I don't think I told you this. When Alex and I first figured out what we stumbled across in the DARPA documents we had a debate about what we would call it when we dropped the tech on the world. Well, it wasn't a debate so much as a conversation mostly between me and myself. I told Alex I thought Winking made a lot of sense but ultimately decided on Blinking because it sounded better to me."

"Then why aren't we going in front of Congress to talk about Blink tech tomorrow?" Sanderson asked.

"Because Alex. Right before we did the dump, he changed the name to Wink just to mess with me." Chris laughed and settled into a smile as he remembered the moment he realized Alex had changed the name on him. Sanderson laughed too.

"That's friends for you." Sanderson said, still smiling.

Victor Chambers (1)

Regulating Chaos

I knew the world would shift when I saw what the hackers, Lax and Lad, had plundered from our systems. My immediate reaction was panic, as of course it should be for the person in charge of a secret program run by the Defense Advanced Research Projects Agency (DARPA). Our office was on technological lockdown before the hack, but it's hard to protect against stupid. Password security was a big part of our annual cybersecurity training and, for god's sake, IT administrators should know better than to use ridiculously obvious passwords, but I guess doctors make the worst patients sometimes. Sitting at my desk, watching the email chain unfold and waiting for the call from my higher-ups, I came to a realization. Screw it! The information was out there. It was big, dangerous content, and it was in the world now. There was no way to unring that bell. All we could hope to do is contain the problem and stay on top of the media. I was sure I would have to fall on my sword for the leak, but I didn't need to make it easy.

In the moments before the Under Secretary of Defense called, I decided to own the leak and stick with my beliefs. The government exists for the people and anything the government owns is really the property of its people. When the information leaked, it leaked to the rightful owners of the property. I understood the need for secrecy, but I wouldn't consider it a disaster for the information to be in the universe, no matter how hard "leadership" came down on me. I could find another job. Hell, I probably had a decent shot of doing the talk show circuit to talk about the leaked tech. I could at least make it interesting. And I did. I refused to condemn the technology that came to be known as Winking. Sure, the hackers were guilty of theft, but the American public were the beneficiaries of the tech, and I let the world know as I bounced from hearings to talk shows to defense department meetings. I even testified in the sentencing hearing of the two hackers who had made it into my systems. I am sure it was a surprise to the leadership when I didn't push for a harsh punishment for the hackers, but they were just kids and I had made my position clear. I repeated the same lines over and over, and held my ground in the certainty that I would be canned at any moment. Oddly, the moment never came. At first, I think, it was because they needed me to explain the Tech and help with the containment strategy. By the time things had settled, a new administration had taken over who valued my approach and wanted me to be part of the Wink team which somehow included one of the hackers who stole the information in the first place.

In the first days of Wink's release, the administration was convinced the best strategy was to put the cat back in the bag. Of course, they weren't successful. Once information is out in the world it is nearly impossible to pull it back and the Wink tech had the advantage of being extremely useful. It didn't take long for the less savory elements of society to take advantage of the Wink tech. Drug cartels bought 3-D printers, hired technical consultants, and set up a drug network that was nearly impossible to stop. Bringing opium in from Afghanistan was simple when the border to the United States did not need to be crossed. It was a matter of having a wink station near the processing facility and another at the distribution location. There were Wink distribution hubs in most cities. They were in apartments, in the middle of forested areas, in basements, nearly everywhere. As a reaction to the lack of security, the administration acted to slow down the spread of the Wink Tech. They only saw the negatives and not the possibilities the tech presented. They sent messages through all the major news channels that labeled the tech as unstable, though there wasn't any real evidence of risk in the building or assembly of the Wink units. An incorrectly assembled Wink unit would just fail to work, but when correctly assembled, the function was consistent and reliable. The President issued an executive order outlawing the Wink tech, which was doomed to be overturned in court. Before the courts could weigh in, the executive order carried the force of law and was rationalized to the American people as a measure meant to protect from the dangerous new technology. In reality it was a matter of control. The consensus was that if the Tech was allowed to spread without control the national system of laws would be tested to the extreme. National security would be impossible and a variety of crimes would be untraceable.

Hawkish members of the President's cabinet warned him that more than drugs would come across the border. Dirty bombs, illegal immigrants and bootlegged products would flood into the country. There was hardly a law they couldn't rationalize as being assisted by the Wink technology. Murders could be committed by anyone in the world. Anyone in the world would have the "opportunity," which would take away a key tool in the toolboxes of investigators. Robbing a house would be much easier if you just plant a Wink unit in the location being robbed. Corporate espionage, tax evasion, human trafficking...everything was helped by instant, untrackable access.

Oddly, the American people seemed to be staying away from using Wink Tech. It may have been the result of the fear mongering in combination with the limited access to 3-D printers. The government had asked industry to pause 3-D printer sales and manufacturing while the technology was still a fringe, niche market populated by technophiles and entrepreneurs. It bought us time. The first thing I was asked to do was to discover a way to track Winks. The ideal was to understand the originating location and the destination, but in a pinch the administration would be happy with either.

It was a fool's errand, really. I said to the assembled staff, "You are talking about attempting to track something moving just below the speed of light. The units only activate for a moment, to top it off. It would be like being in an airplane and someone flickering a laser pointer at you for an instant, then trying to locate the person on the ground. Sure, given the perfect circumstances we might get it right once in a while, but the effort would be outrageous and to track the Wink movement at scale would be ridiculously expensive."

I told them the solution was in a different direction. I had picked the idea up from then Senator Sanderson. Don't stop it, control it. Find a way to get the technology to be built with tracking capabilities that would be automatically reported. GPS for the tech. Make sure we have trusted manufacturers who build the product cheap enough and well enough that it would be silly to use a 3-D printer at home. Subsidize the production if they couldn't get the price down. Become the leaders and dominate the industry and do it quickly before competing countries ended up in the mix.

The administration at the time was not interested, but they were doomed in the next election cycle for so many reasons, not the least of which was Sanderson eating their lunch with Wink Tech idealism. Sanderson got a hold of my conversations with the administration; the President's cabinet was leaky. They were as porous as the borders had become. There were tapes of me making pitches to the President. I sounded fiery and contrary. I think Sanderson liked it. He called me early after his election and asked me to join his crew, which I enthusiastically accepted. It was like being part of the heist team in an Ocean's movie. We were making lemonade out of the lemons, and it was invigorating. New tech, new opportunities and a new administration who seemed determined to make the most of the tech in exactly the way that sounded best to me. They had the American people in mind the whole time and wanted to keep America on top, king of the hill, as the Tech became a mainstay of life around the world.

When the change to the Sanderson administration was complete the extent of the problems associated with the previous president's attempts to control the tech became clear and the path to fixing the underlying issues became less clear. The black markets around the country had exploded. Everything was bleeding through the borders as if the borders didn't exist, because by and large they didn't. Counterfeit goods, drugs, people, weapons, even uncontrolled daily use products like maple syrup from Canada and champagne from France were available in cities throughout the country. The empirical evidence showed the impact. Drug impounds were up seven hundred percent compared to the period before the launch of the Wink tech. Knock-off goods were being confiscated at a rate that was hard to even track.

An interesting side effect was tax and levy arbitrage were making a new class of entrepreneurs around the world. Cigarettes from Kyrgyzstan, which were purchased for a fifth of the cost in the US, were brought into the country and sold on the streets for a premium. The open borders were redistributing wealth around the world. It was an experiment in free market trade. The volume of Wink units in the world wasn't out of control, but it was large enough and America was at the center of the profit seeking with its high disposable income and strong propensity to spend.

In an early meeting of the Wink Commission, as we came to be called, we decided action was needed in a hurry. Each piece of the puzzle had to be addressed: the black market, the drug trade, human trafficking, tax evasion, and the lack of quality and purity standards in products.

During the meeting, we heard from a variety of sources. The D.C. police chief talked about the increase in drug trafficking in his city. A Hollywood executive described the lost revenue from bootlegged DVDs flooding the streets from China and Russia. Probably the most interesting conversation we had was with the Commissioner of the IRS. His name was Richard Keeting. Lean and bookish, he clumsily carried a comical ski-slope diagram on a large piece of poster board into the room and sat it on the marker ledge of the dry erase board that was positioned at the front of the conference room we occupied that day. He sat his bag down, took a really long, deep breath and said, "Well, I hope we can afford this room in the next couple of years."

There wasn't really any laughter from the group because it was one of those jokes that you can't tell is really a joke until after you catch the context of the next paragraph. Keeting said, "Fine, I'm not making any more jokes," and flashed a quick smile. "Here's the issue. I have been tracking tax revenues across the country for a little while now and have noticed a trend. I bet you can guess what it is." He looked around the room waiting for a response.

I said, "There's less?"

"Spot on." He turned to his poster and said, "I was going to ask if you ever played that Chutes and Ladders game when you were a kid. You know they call it Snakes and Ladders in England. Who's sliding down snakes? Anyway, this isn't the ladder. It's the chute, and we are sliding down it. The problem isn't really at the federal level. We get our revenue from income and payroll taxes. The problem is at the state level. We're seeing a decline in sales tax across the states, especially in the states where the sales tax is particularly high like California." He turned back to his graph and said, "This isn't really a graph of sales tax. I brought it in for effect. But still, we have seen a two percent decline in sales tax. That sounds a lot less sexy. Do you know how much a two percent decline in sales tax costs the United States in a year?" Keeting looked around the room, we looked at each other and there was a general shaking of heads. "Eight billion dollars!" Keeting paused for dramatic effect.

"I don't really get it. It's still only two percent." said the Secretary of the Interior, who was part of the commission.

"Ahhh!" Keeting said, pointing his finger to the ceiling. "That's just it! It's two percent now and Wink tech is just rolling out. Imagine what happens when it is universal. States won't be able to fund themselves. There will be state bankruptcies around the country. Now the federal government has a problem. We'll have to bail them out. We can't have all the state bond issuances in default. As it is, a two percent decline might be more than some states can absorb. Then what?"

"So, what are you suggesting?" asked the secretary.

"Oh, I'm not suggesting anything. That's your problem. I just thought you should know. Did you know that some states don't have any sales tax? What happens if people start grocery shopping in states where they don't have tax and just Wink home with their groceries? If Winking is ubiquitous, we will have a real reckoning coming."

"Well then, who do we talk to about making sure we don't have your 'reckoning' then?" asked Chris Stevens, who had been appointed to the committee by President Sanderson. "If President Sanderson wants to push for legalization and ubiquity, we need to be prepared."

Keeting looked grave. "Here's the deal. You probably need a team. Some economists, an ethicist or two, some business folks, and a few politicians for good measure. Politicians love committees. You should make a committee. I hate committees. The original idea was good. Did you know committees were formed in the U.S. for the first time during the revolution to drum up anti-British sentiment and help push the U.S. to independence? Good stuff ...action oriented. Committees are where ideas go to die. You guys are better off just figuring out a strategy for yourself and seeing if President Sanderson has the political muscle to make it work. Tell you what, I'll stick around if you guys want to work it out now." He set his stuff down on the floor again, after having started making his move to the door, and put his arms on the conference table with his chin in his hands. He quietly waited for the flabbergasted room to reply.

I jumped in, "Well, seeing as though we don't have a ton of time for decision making, now is as good a time as any. Anyone have any ideas?"

The work coming out of the small group was amazingly productive. Maybe it was the fact that no one in the room, apart from Keeting, had any real idea of how to build fiscal policy or maybe it was the group dynamic. There were a lot of interesting personalities and skill sets. Ideas bounced around until we settled on a solution that seemed to get the least number of deep sighs from Keeting and made the rest of the group smile. I can't recall who came up with the name but it was a general hit the second it was said out loud. We would call it 'Winkome Tax'. We just needed to figure out how to make it work.

The idea behind Winkome tax was this: We couldn't really tax people's purchases when the whole world became their shopping centers, and we would likely lose control over a chunk of property and payroll taxes since the world was about to open up to residing and working anywhere without restriction.

What we could do was tax people's Winks from location to location. To do that, we would need to control the industry. We needed the solution I had shot down as part of the prior administration, but it was clearly a necessity now. The main problem being we couldn't, at the time, figure out who was Winking where or when. In the course of the meeting, a cell phone rang and was quickly clicked off. Keeting, in typical knowledge share mode, told us cell tech and Wink tech had a lot in common and cell companies figured out how to track call information with a system of hubs and technology in the phones. Chris said, "Why not do the same with Winking?"

The Secretary of the Interior jumped in and said, "We create hubs for Wink traffic? You mean like Wink train stations? And then what?"

"That and more," said Chris. "Sure, stations are good, but what if we made the tracking software required on all Wink units?"

"How can we enforce that when people can print a Wink unit in their garage?" the Interior Secretary asked.

It hit me like a two-ton anvil and I said, "A person could make a cell phone in the garage too, if they had enough tools and knowledge, but they generally don't. They don't because it would be a pain and there are already companies out there that do it well. Really well. The cell phone companies have it figured out. Every year they release a new phone with features - security features and usage features. We are all locked into the cycle. We get a new phone and stay connected to the service distribution network. We need to do the same with Winking. Then we can tax the devices and their usage just like we do with gasoline." Eyes in the room brightened and Chris named it at that moment. "We can call it Winkome tax." Chris said and the room laughed. Over the next few hours, a general plan was formed that stayed almost completely intact at the time of launch.

In the months that followed, we put the ideas in action. We decided there was a need to get the Wink tech out to the world at a price point that was cheap enough people would buy rather than build. For the vast majority of people in the country, the idea of buying 3-D printing equipment, learning to program, and print their own Wink unit was naturally prohibitive. I mean, who wants to put in the effort? So, in the early days we were competing against people who owned and understood the necessary tech and were selling their builds on the black market. It wasn't a giant community at the time, it was a niche market, but had space to grow in a hurry. We cut the knees out of the process with a full court press.

The rights to Wink tech needed to be doled out. We decided to select a few companies who met a short list of criteria: they had to be heavily impacted by the proliferation of the new tech, have strong production capacity or enough scale and agility to build the capacity in a hurry, and be big enough they could hurt the American economy if they failed. The hard part was knowing some companies would still get left in the dust. Still, we had to choose and the companies were eager. Ford, General Motors, American Airlines and Southwest Airlines were all tapped. We asked that they quickly ramp up production and work on a development cycle to ensure new product features to keep consumers locked into the buy cycle.

A few months into the work with the four launch companies, it was clear the two airlines would need help and time to get production underway and the two car companies were slow to convert production. They were all moving at the same, slow pace, which we couldn't afford. It was President Sanderson's idea to give them a little healthy competition to scare them into production. Sanderson was close with the CEO at the Alphabet Corporation who owned Google and gave them the chance to jump in. Jump in they did. Google was in production within a month. They presented their marketing campaign, new security features, and distribution plan in a producers meeting. It scared the pants off the original four, who were not so naive to think they would survive a Wink revolution being pushed by a tech giant who was committed. The original four companies knew if they missed this window, they would need to plan on ever-declining market share until they disappeared into oblivion. The CEOs of the four went back to their companies, hired consultants, brought in partners and were actively participating in the market only a few weeks later.

There were five companies all competing for a share in a trillion-dollar market. They fought hard to gain position, which meant heavy marketing, low prices and ubiquitous distribution. It meant a pace of expansion for Wink tech the likes of which no tech had rivaled.

We beat the curve. All the Wink units sold across the globe contained tracking software that was ready for the Winkome tax. We were just waiting for the tech to take full hold in the marketplace, then we could turn on the tax. Until then, we had to contend with the horrible problem of drug markets exploding around the country. No borders meant free flowing products. Battles between rival drug gangs around the country were popping up on American streets in places where drug violence was completely foreign and people were feeling insecure. A new strategy was needed but nothing was readily apparent. I mean, how do you stop something that could pop up anywhere at any time when you had no way of tracking across a nation with 3.8 million square miles? I guess the answer would be you don't.

Remember the "Just Say No" campaign from the 1980s? How did that work out? Well, that was the plan again. We needed to control the drug markets on the demand side. The supply side was uncontrollable. I remember reading an article about how the D.A.R.E. program actually increased drug usage by something like 30% for those kids who were in the program and a bunch more ended up smokers. Basically, the program made them more aware of their options. It was an advertising campaign and it helped kids get the street lingo down. Not to mention the program helped a generation of people associate drug addiction with criminal behavior rather than illness. Without many other options, we were stuck trying to improve a program whose outcomes were dubious at best.

The Wink Committee ended up calling our new program "Don't Dare." We focused our attention on treatment for addiction and when we educated children about drug use, our focus was on real world examples of how drugs could ruin lives with survivors of addiction running the show. We also spent billions of dollars, which were starting to get harder to find, on alternative programs to keep youth engaged in other activities. I never really felt like our programs could make a huge impact, but we had to do something and, I guess, with the benefit of hindsight we saw success. The rate of drug use was flat to slightly down, even though there was a multifold increase in the supply.

Not surprisingly, a lot of the innovation with the tech happened in the military sector. We weren't part of that development, but President Sanderson asked a representative of the Joint Chiefs and a representative for the Director of National Intelligence to keep our committee in the loop in case we could use their development in our area.

A year after the formation of the committee, we had a debrief meeting with representatives from national intelligence, the military, and the director of DARPA, my old stomping grounds. The development work was moving at a fever pitch. There was a real sense of creativity and dynamism in the inventions coming from all corners of the defense complex. General Jennine McCullough, the Chief of Staff of the Army, was the first to present as a representative of the joint chiefs. She was quick to smile, seemed confident and well prepared. She was very much in the mold of military precision with her clothes perfectly pressed and her papers laid on the table in front of her just so. Her pen was set perfectly parallel next to her notepad and her supporting documents were in a stack to the side, perfectly stapled in the top corner. She didn't rise to speak and didn't waste time with greetings, the introductions having been made when she entered.

"I'll start us off. The military has been focused on the scaling problem in order to move equipment to zones of operation around the world more effectively. We want to Wink a tank in and out of the field in an instant. The obvious problem is the standard Wink Specs are human sized. It can only Wink objects slightly wider and slightly taller than a human. The limitation was determined to be due to the size of the Wink Pad and not due to technological limitations. Larger Wink Pads means the ability to Wink larger objects. Still, the delivery of a Pad large enough to transport a tank into an active war zone is tricky. Our first thought was to build them then airdrop them in bulk to a forward position. It worked. We had success, but it certainly wasn't ideal. Our next advance came in materials. We were able to make Wink Pads out of a flexible conductive material weave containing carbon fiber and graphene. This diagram shows our newest Wink Pads." General McCullough handed a stack of pages to the representative from national intelligence who was seated on her right, who then took a page and passed it along around the table.

The document showed images for two designs. The first was like a large Chinese folding fan with two rigid poles that when pulled apart formed a circular Wink Pad. The second was a more complex spiral shape.

General McCullough began again. "The first shape you see was based on those fans we used to get in dollar stores as kids. The materials we used to build were extremely light and we were able to carry two long poles with the newly created Wink material, which we called Wink Fiber, gathered in the middle. The two poles were hinged at the bottom and could be pulled apart to make a large pad. The problem was that the diameter of the circular pad was always twice the length of the poles. For something really large, we would need pretty large poles. The second image you see was the improvement. We stole the idea from NASA's folding Starshade. The circle in this image is relatively compact and spiraled. When you tug the two sides of the disc, the circle spirals open to five hundred percent of its compact size and can be packed into large backpacks. The packs, as seen here, are just over 6 feet in diameter, but when unloaded make a circle with a diameter of 33 feet which is conveniently the length of an M1A1 tank. Basically, a trooper with a slightly oversized backpack can carry a tank into battle."

"That's amazing, have you used it in the field?" asked the Secretary of the Interior.

"We are still in testing, but there have been no adverse tests to date," said the General.

"Are there any limits to the size? I mean, how big could you go?" Chris asked

"We have not seen any limits on size. We don't see any reason we couldn't go with a three-hundred-foot diameter." General McCullough, with obvious enthusiasm, showed a fast smile. If you could make a pad big enough, you could Wink in a whole barracks full of soldiers.

When I was a kid in school, particularly in science class, I would get in trouble for not paying attention. My teachers thought it was because I didn't care about what they were talking about, but the truth was that I would follow what they were saying and my mind would wander with ideas. Conversations about Newton's laws would lead me down a path. If force is equal to mass times acceleration, then if you could accelerate something fast enough, you would need barely any mass for it to be full of power. My brain would jump from idea to idea. Like how the Flash should be the most powerful superhero in the universe because he could accelerate his finger fast enough, a flick could take out superman. Then I would think about how tiny objects in space moving at ridiculously high speeds could take down a space station or how powerful a rail gun might be. Getting the debrief on how Wink was being used put me into the same spiral. I lost my connection to the conversation. Loosely in the background, I heard the general say things like how they were working on smaller Wink Units that could be used for troop resupply, but my mind wandered to a soldier sitting behind a covered position, holding an empty magazine for his rifle, out of ammunition, starting to panic. Then he pulls out his small folding Wink Unit that was tucked into his rucksack and calls for a restock of ammo. Instantly, a stack of magazines appears and he's saved. Then I follow the thought down the rabbit hole. What if we could make a Wink Unit small enough and flexible enough to fit into a wallet that used some of the same folding tech the general discussed earlier. You would never need to carry lunch with you to work. You could walk to a park near your office, have a craving for a Philly cheesesteak, order a sandwich from Geno's in Philly and have it delivered right to your pocket device. The Wallet Wink and cell phone would be all you really needed to carry. Everything would be close at hand. Companies would be formed who did nothing but specialize in the delivery of items to people around the world. It would be instant Amazon, and it would be ubiquitous, forget delivery drones and drivers. Competition would keep prices low since the cost of delivery would be near zero. Would that have an impact on the economy? It would likely cause deflation in a hurry, but what about unemployment?

I snapped out of my reverie to find the general had finished her update. I was sure I missed something interesting and made a note to check with Chris after the presentations to get caught up. General McCullogh passed the talking stick to the gentleman on her right from national intelligence. He was a heavy man with a thick voice. He must have gained weight recently since his shirt didn't seem to fit his neck. He had the top button unbuttoned and the tie pulled up high in an attempt to hide it.

"My name is Donald Johnson. Don't laugh. I go by Donald, and I am guessing you know why. My role is liaison between the intelligence apparatuses of the United States and various organizations that have been deemed vital to our intelligence work," he said without a smile in what seemed to be some well-rehearsed sentences. Then under his breath he added, "or anyone the president has added to the list." He garumphed as he cleared his throat and began again. "Our work has largely been in the area of tracking the act of Winking. The previous administration's Wink tracking priority persisted to the new administration. We went for some time without progress, but a couple months back we received a call from MIT about something they noticed in their work with LIGO. LIGO is The Laser Interferometer Gravitational-Wave Observatory. There are observatories in Washington and Louisiana. They were picking up a lot of noise in their sensory equipment, and it seemed to be correlated to the increased Wink traffic. While we haven't yet been able to narrow down specific traffic, it seems clear we can detect the traffic. The LIGO stations are large and expensive, and it takes multiple stations to identify the direction of the traffic and it would likely take three stations to pinpoint a location, but at least we can say we found a clear possibility for detection. We are in the refinement stages at this point and hope to build a large working model that can be reduced in both size and cost."

I was curious about the tech we had released to date and whether we had planned well enough with our tracking protocols, so I asked, "Donald, do you have a sense if they will be able to decipher the differences between our tracked signals and unlicensed travel?"

"It's too early to tell," he responded. "One of the scientists we spoke to suggested we bury a code in our licensed transmissions. We may eventually need to synchronize our efforts but we are very early in the process."

The remaining efforts from the intelligence community were focused on incursion and the placement of spy assets and equipment. There was nothing terribly novel, but it was clear they were embracing the tech. When he was done speaking, the room was quiet for a heartbeat, quiet enough to hear another thick breath from Donald Johnson as he shuffled in his chair uncomfortably. I noticed I wasn't the only one who had let their attention lapse. People were doodling and checking their phones.

I somehow hadn't really taken notice of the last speaker, the DARPA Director who occupied my old position. In hindsight, I can't believe she didn't capture my attention immediately considering she has occupied my thoughts nearly every day since. When I did see her, I really saw her. She was slender with dark olive skin, jet black hair, and a mouth that seemed to smile while it was at rest. Her eyes smiled with her mouth as if they were connected, the look was maddening. I had to make an honest effort to avoid gawking.

"Well, hello all. I am Saraswati Singh. I am the recently appointed acting director of DARPA. I have been intrigued to hear about the developments in the other areas and unsurprisingly, we have been working on many of the same things." She flashed a smile that brought her already smile-leaning face to a new level that could only be described as sunshine. I was done. Her voice lilted beautifully as she spoke, her English proper, her pronunciation precise. She continued, "One area we have been pursuing is Wink Travel with no end point. As I am sure you are all aware, the current state of Wink Tech requires both a sending and receiving terminal which dramatically reduces the applications of the technology. The main purposes of the receiving unit are that it creates a clearly defined location in three-dimensional space and assists with reconstitution of the transferred object. If we are able to solve both the reconstitution and location problems, we would be able to transport people just as they did in Star Trek." Again, she smiled. This time, my heart skipped. As far back as I can recall, my heart would skip beats. When I was younger it worried me, but the doctors assured me the skipped beats were normal, that a lot of people experienced the skips, particularly with heavy caffeine or stress. At that instant, when the new director of DARPA spoke my heart skipped at the same time I exhaled and, in the moment, it felt like my last breath and my first breath.

I had a compulsive need to speak to her directly. "Ms. Singh, have you made any progress in either area?" I asked, fully aware I was interrupting and sure she was going to get to their progress shortly.

"Please call me Sara." My mind registered a connection, she was Sara, pronounced like star-a. Cheesy, but a clear representation of where my head was at that moment. "We have made significant progress on the location issue by using the array of units around the world and our satellite technology to make a sort of net around the planet. There are still challenges in areas where there is low Wink Unit coverage, which represent the areas of our planet with lower populations or lower socio-economic standing. The bigger challenge is the reconstitution issue. We are stalled in that area, though we have many brilliant scientists at work on the problem. We see the continued efforts in that area as an opportunity to expand our space program to include star systems within a reasonable distance to Earth."

Victor Chambers (2)

The World on Fire

Monthly debrief meetings with the military and intelligence communities continued for some time after the initial debrief, but attendance waned. In typical governmental fashion, after the second meeting yielded no new information, the original participants sent subordinates to take their place. Sara attended through the third meeting, but I failed to make a connection. It wasn't for a lack of trying. It was for a lack of effectiveness. I talked to her at every opportunity, but was too anxious, nerdy, and hapless to actually ask her out on a date. Somehow it always seemed inappropriate to "chat her up" during a work function. Then at the fourth meeting she was no longer present. I stuck it out for two more meetings hoping she would show, but she didn't.

A few months after I stopped attending, I got a call from President Sanderson to meet him at the White House. I had been to the White House before under the previous administration. Somehow the building felt different when I visited President Sanderson. Under the prior president the building had a haunting, suspicious feel. It was somehow darker and more foreboding, but with President Sanderson at the helm, I walked the halls and felt more at home. It was likely just my imagination and the fact that Sanderson and I saw eye to eye on most things. It might also have had something to do with Sanderson's folksy hometown feel and the homier decorations around the house.

I was led to the Oval Office for our discussion. The broad windows behind the president's desk were directly in front of me as I walked through the door. Once on the other side of the door, I stood near the entry way as I waited to be acknowledged. President Sanderson asked the room to be cleared so he and I could talk privately which resulted in a staffer and two members of the Secret Service exiting and the door being closed behind them. Sanderson motioned for me to sit on one of the cream-colored sofas in the middle of the room as he smiled and set himself on the other sofa.

Sanderson smiled as if he was on the inside of an inside joke that I was unlikely to ever be part of. "Victor, nice to see you again. How are things? Are you getting along okay with the committee?"

"Things are really good. I feel like we are doing good work together, and I'm pretty sure we've made a difference in the direction of the Wink Tech around the world, but I am betting you didn't call me in for a status check."

"Well then, I guess we're getting right to it." Sanderson leaned in and smiled showing his nearly perfect pearly whites. "I thought I was plucking this chicken, but maybe you are. Okay, here's the deal. We're putting together a new task force with the goal of being first to stand up a base on the moon. The Europeans, Indians, Japanese, Russians, Chinese, and the United Arab Emirates all have dogs in the hunt, and I want us to get that rabbit first. Time's running thin though, and I think large teams end up preventing quick movement. So, we're going with a four-person team, and we want as much knowledge about Wink Tech as we can muster. The goal is to be on a rocket that's heading to the moon in three months. We contracted with Orbital Systems, they're the winner of the Lunar Lander Challenge XPRIZE. They're a small team, and the leader is pretty quirky, but they managed to build a functional prototype that is basically ready to relaunch in three months. It's a big responsibility. What do you think? Are you in?"

"What do I think?" I was preening myself, straightening my jacket and preparing for a moment I had been waiting for most of my life. "I think you couldn't keep me away! You know, this was the kind of thing that attracted me to DARPA in the first place. I am in...100%, but can I ask a favor?"

"Don't see why not. Shoot." Sanderson was genuinely intrigued. I could see it in his eyes.

"Saraswati Singh. I met her in our debrief meetings with military and intelligence communities. She seems to have a great grasp of the tech and really creative mind. Can we pull her into the group? I know you said four people, and you probably have already identified everyone, but maybe consider a fifth?" I definitely showed my hand with the last bit. I heard my words rattle around my head as I said them. In the echo, I heard a desperate man and I was sure the President of the United States, the most powerful man in the world, heard it as well. I was instantly embarrassed, which historically wasn't easy for me. The truth was I was acting on impulse. I wasn't thinking. It was like my mouth started moving before I consciously realized what I was asking but the truth of it wasn't lost on me.

Sanderson's smile was so big it spread to my face. We were both sitting there smiling at each other like a couple high school boys passing notes about a girl, and Sanderson said, "I sure do have some funny news for you. The reason you're here is because Sara asked for you. It sounds like you two are on the same page. If you want the advice of an old man, get that fish on a hook." We both laughed and dispensed with business. We spent the rest of our meeting just catching up on life, drinking tea and sharing a laugh. President Sanderson was really a wonder. He was quick witted, a genius at listening and you could feel his heart when he talked. No wonder he made it into the highest office in the land.

The committee was made up of me and Sara, an Egyptian scientist who was a transplant to the U.S. named Babu Gamal, and the head of the Jet Propulsion Laboratory and the California Institute of Technology's space program, Simon Warren. It was an amazing amount of skill and knowledge for such a small group and it left me feeling outclassed. Gamal had experience in exoplanetary geography, exoplanetary atmospheric conditions, the identification and use of planetary materials and a strong foundation in lunar exploration having participated in the Indian Space Research Organization's moon probe that successfully fulfilled their mission the year before. Warren was a powerhouse in physics, the motion of astronomical bodies, spacecraft engineering and had also recently taken part in the successful landing of another probe on Mars called Quest. I was there as an invite and wasn't sure what I would bring to the table.

I was a civil engineer by training and joined the Army Corps of Engineers early in my career. My father was in the Corps, and it seemed to be a big part of his identity. So, the Army Corps of Engineers held an attraction for me that went beyond its mission of helping people. I was part of a lot of projects from disaster relief, to construction, to ecological management. The diversity of projects was interesting and I enjoyed managing them. Moving people and resources was where I shined. I transferred through the ranks until I was promoted to the Chief of Staff position for the Corps. I then transferred into a deputy director position at DARPA and eventually the director. It was never my technical acumen that got me recognized. Instead, it was my ability to organize, execute, and come in under budget. In my eyes, and particularly for this team, that made me a bureaucrat in a room full of technocrats. The anxiety of engaging with the group made me feel like a freshman in a room full of seniors.

The first meeting was by far the most productive, not surprisingly. The start of any project was like that for me. All the energy and ideas tended to come out at the beginning and from there it was just putting meat on bone. Generally, most people are good at beginnings, some people are good at endings, but there are only a few who are good at the middle bits. I guess that's where I excel, the relentless drive through the middle. I was the beefy running back pushing the ball down field a little bit at a time.

Sara kicked off the first meeting. She said, "Hello gentlemen, we are lucky enough to come together with a specific objective which looks to be well within our reach. The president requested that I pull together a small team to deliver this objective. Each of you has a skill set that shall be crucial for this work." It was likely just my insecurity, but I felt like that line was directed to me.

"Together, we will find a way to bring the United States back to the moon within the shortest time frame imaginable. In addition, we will set up a station and lay claim to areas on the moon of strategic importance. One key objective is to have a base near Clavius Crater in order to secure the water resources which seem available in the area. Are the objectives clear to this team? If so, we can do introductions and begin." The room generally nodded to confirm understanding and the day began.

We worked thirteen hours that day, though the work wasn't tiring. Ideas flew around, and I settled into a sense that I could contribute. The highlight of my engagement was when we were discussing how to get building materials to the moon. I had a brain wave, and I blurted out the idea before I realized I had it. It was like my mouth was moving before my brain could catch up. Sara had mentioned the work we heard about through our meetings with the military and intelligence community. She mentioned the miniaturization work, and I drifted off thinking about the tank winking into existence next to a soldier who was winking mortars to himself on his smaller Wink Pad. The idea of a Russian nesting doll of Wink units made me smile. I said, "Here's a thought. What if we used the military tech in a different way? We send up a human sized Wink Unit to the moon, then we send up an astronaut with a larger unfolding Wink Unit, then another even larger unit and so on until we have one on the moon that would be large enough to house a small base. We can build the base here on Earth and just wink the whole thing to the moon."

Simon Warren added on, "You know. That makes a lot of sense. We won't need the infrastructure to build on the moon at all. We can test the whole thing safely on Earth while the Wink unit is delivered to our location or even locations on the moon. We know how to work drones and land safely. That would be all we would need at this stage, or at least by the three-month launch window. No off-planet construction. I guess the question is, can we make a moon base-sized Wink pad? Well, actually two."

"I think we can. We have gone larger than tanks already and the folding techniques allow them to be unfolded very cleverly. The new fabrics in use by the military makes it relatively light and transportable." Sara said, grinning, and she shot me a glance that said, "Well done," and melted my heart again. I could die happy.

"Well, we have our locations, our techniques, and a rocket to send up our equipment. Some testing will be needed to ensure we can connect the Wink devices over such a distance. We may not have to worry much about the base location, since we will have someone on the moon scouting for suitable locations," Babu added in his barely accented English. "This works!" He gave an audible whoop. "Might I suggest a mission name?"

"Of course," Sara answered immediately.

"There is an Egyptian god whose name translates to traveler and is the god of the moon. Khonshu. I suggest we call this project Khonshu and perhaps we can call the rover that places the initial Wink unit "Traveler?" Babu added.

"Exquisite!" said Simon. Sara and I agreed and so was born Project Khonshu.

We broke ourselves into working teams to handle the various aspects of the build. Sara was tasked with ensuring we were able to build a Wink unit large enough to handle an entire base. Simon worked on the orbital craft and landing equipment. Babu focused on the landing site and the construction of the Earth base that would be Winked to the moon, though the base was really a collaborative effort between Simon and Babu. My role was twofold. The first was to act as a general project manager which meant tracking progress, managing the regular status update meetings, and clearing any obstacles that arose. The second was to liaise between the group and our rocket partners at Orbital Systems and particularly our relationship with Steve Angelo. The second part of my assignment turned out to be the bigger workload.

Angelo was a tech billionaire turned space enthusiast. He was short, a little stocky, and he always dressed in his "uniform" of jeans and gray hooded sweatshirt. To his credit, he was able to build a reusable rocket that could make it to the moon and back consistently and he had proven it a dozen or more times before our mission. The media loved him. They could count on his larger-than-life personality to draw viewers and if they kept him talking long enough he would say something that would make headlines. He came across as a genius but not the kind you wanted to hang around. He was more like a great white shark, majestic but best kept at a distance. I did my research on him before I met him based on Simon Warren's guidance. Simon suggested I should "find out what I am in for to minimize the shock of transition." Simon had worked with him in his role at JPL and seemed less than eager to work with him again.

"He's obsessive, which has made him successful. It's a trait you want under the right circumstances. It can be a lot to handle in day-to-day life," Simon told me. From what I was able to glean from Angelo's interviews and company speeches, his obsession in his early career was coding and image recognition which led him, and some fellow college students, to build an application that allowed an artificial intelligence algorithm to decipher the contents of a picture. They sold the technology to a large technology firm for way too much money and it became a staple codebase for facial recognition software, image search tools on the internet and a variety of other applications. Angelo took his winnings and moved on to form his own company that focused on space. His new obsession was the moon. He wanted to own it, to the extent that was possible. His vision was a craft that could easily traverse the distance between Earth and the moon, carrying passengers to stay at his moon resort. Watching the interviews left me with the distinct impression that he wanted to start his own moon colony that wasn't subject to the governments of earth. A colony where he was the king and the rules were his to make. His anti-government streak was obvious in his rhetoric, but even more obvious in the name of his yacht, which he called "The Ungoverned" and was kept in international waters for a substantial part of the year.

Even after all of my preparation, I wasn't really ready to meet the famous Steve Angelo. Angelo was the type of guy who talked to hear himself talk. He didn't talk to you so much as he talked *at* you. Which, if your goal is to get to know him and understand him, is pretty convenient, but if your goal is to get him to reach a point or come to a conclusion you were out of luck. Our first interaction took place at his facility outside Las Vegas, Nevada, which was really just an oversized storage unit with a variety of technical equipment strewn about. The main differences between Orbital Systems' building and any run of the mill storage facility were the height of the ceilings and the large craft lying prone in the middle. They were immense since they needed to accommodate the height of the rockets. I found it impossible to enter the building and not look directly up to see the magnitude of the complex. When I walked through the main door, I was greeted by what must have been a government liaison officer who was likely alerted to my arrival when I passed through the security gates. There was no use in her efforts since my attention was solidly elsewhere as I marveled at the scale. I felt her trying to talk to me about the agenda for the day, and I tried not to be rude, but it was difficult for me to be on task. As it was, she left almost no impression on me. I think I may have at least said, "Pleased to meet you" as my eyes wandered.

I was drifting forward, looking around lost in my thoughts when Angelo joined us and relieved the poor ignored greeter. He set his hand on her shoulder and looked at her with a smile and she caught on that she was dismissed. He turned his smile to me and said, "Pretty amazing, isn't it? I feel like it's as close to being outdoors as you can get while being indoors. It's a haven for the claustrophobic of the world. You must be Victor Chambers?" He reached a hand out to me.

I took his hand and found myself in his oddly strong, mildly aggressive grip. I found out later from Sara that Mr. Angelo liked to give a good squeeze in all of his handshakes. She admitted to a slightly sore hand after their meeting. It must have been a way of exerting his authority or maybe he just lacked basic human empathy, either way it didn't set me at ease. "Guilty as charged." I said withdrawing my hand and pocketing it.

"Well, thanks for coming to visit. I was told the goal for today was to see the progress on the rocket and start to work out the logistics for our 'package' that will be delivered in a couple weeks. There it is but I imagine you didn't miss it."

He gestured at the immense cylinder across the floor of the facility. "Want to get up close and personal with it?" He asked in a conspiratorial whisper.

"That'd be great. I'm all yours," I said and he turned and began walking at an oddly brisk pace as if his goal was to keep me just slightly behind him. As we walked, he pointed out landmarks. It was clear that he lived in the facility. Not only was he familiar with it, he navigated like someone would navigate a tour of their own home when showing guests around for the first time. We walked toward the front of the rocket; which was the section nearest to the entry and the full scale began to take shape in my mind. The building was vast, but the scale was hard to absorb in a single bite. You had to rotate your head around to see the length and breadth and even when you stood next to one of the exterior walls, the building seemed sized appropriately, large but necessarily so. Somehow the lack of columns and walls to support the roof tricked the eyes when you were in the middle. The rocket, on the other hand, could be stood next to in the middle of the room and it gave you a sense of the sheer magnitude of the undertaking. I remembered thinking how amazing humankind is. We were like ants building giant mounds, creating at a scale that far exceeded our own size. It was a cartoon where humans were shrunk and everything around us looked gigantic. I noticed there was a golf cart next to the front of the rocket where we were walking and realized its use. To see what was happening in the facility, we would have to drive. Walking would take too long and be too tiring.

"This is the body. The two boosters, which will attach to the sides of this main fuselage, are over there." Angelo gestured to the farther corners of the plant which was out of site due to building materials blocking the view. "We can likely skip over those since they're less interesting. The real peepshow is here at the head of the rocket. This is where the orbital will be loaded to contain the Wink units."

"I would really like to see all the rocket engines and am particularly interested in the orbital. I understand you have been working with Simon Warren on the build?" I said, feeling like it was my job to act a little like an inspector.

"Have it your way." Angelo said with a quick and nervous-looking smile. "We can head over to the other booster rockets next. First, let's dig around in the cone of the rocket a little. That's where all the fiddly bits are."

We continued our walk over to the orbitals, which were positioned on the other side of the main body of the rocket near the front, which made sense considering they would likely try to assemble it in full in the factory before rolling it outside. The orbital sat in a cordoned off large square in what looked like a crime scene. There was computer equipment on a cart and a few people grouped together, talking and pointing at a panel on the side of the craft. The orbital, which was officially called "Traveller" based on Gamal's suggestion, was a box on stilts. In no way did it resemble something that could actually travel. The miracle of space is that shapes don't matter as much without wind resistance.

"So, this is Traveller. It kind of looks like a fancy shoe box. How is it coming along?" I asked.

"If it's a shoe box, it's the coolest fucking shoe box in the universe." Angelo quipped and he seemed to have the clear intent to injure with his comment since there was no mirth in it, even though he was smiling when he said it. "Think of it as the opposite of one of those $1,000 toilets the government is always buying. We aren't wasting here. We make it as cheap and robust as possible, something NASA could never do. It doesn't need to look pretty. It needs to work."

"Copy that. If it's so well suited to work, what's with its smaller cousin over there?" I pointed on the other side of the Traveller, to the orbitals little brother. They looked the same, apart from the size.

"That's a backup. Fortune favors the prepared. We want to make sure we are ready in time and having a backup rig is a good way to make sure we have something to launch in case we have a failure in the main system." Angelo said.

I asked, "Why smaller then? Shouldn't you have made them the same size?"

"That's in case we need to fit the orbital into the existing housing of the Traveller." Angelo replied.

"Make sense. Does it at least have a name?" I asked

"We call it the Stand-by traveler. We used to call it Stand-by for short, but that somehow got shortened to Stan," Angelo said, clearly amused at their wit. Suddenly the South Park stickers on the computer cart that were connected to "Stan" made sense.

"Redundancy makes sense too. Welp, is there anything you need to get the Traveller and Stan ready for launch in a few short weeks?" I thought trying to be helpful would make the awkward interactions with Angelo a little easier. Mistake.

"What I really need is less of you 'G-men' in my business. We have successfully launched in the past, and we'll do it again. We know what we're doing. Space isn't really the place for governments. It's a place for clever and resourceful people, not bureaucrats." Angelo sneered as he said the last word. He was happy to show his discontent. "Orbital Systems, my company, did it faster, safer, and cheaper than the government ever could. You know what they say: lead, follow, or get out of the way. Well, I'm asking you all to get out of the way."

At that point I wanted to be anyone else but me, and anywhere else but there. "I understand your concern Mr. Angelo. I have a job to do here. I need to make sure we are on target and will be ready. Just like it's your job to make it cheaper, faster, and safer. We are paying you mightily for this project. We have an investment to protect." I tried to say it as kindly as I could but with a clear sense of purpose in the hopes he may respect my role in the situation. Instead, he chuckled at me, and I felt the heat rising in my face and my heart picked up pace a little. "Let's go see the booster rockets. I need to make sure they are on track as well." I said with no small amount of pique and as much authority as I could muster.

While we made our way in relative silence to the second stage rockets, I asked, "How does the Wink pad deploy from the orbital? I didn't see that in the design?" I realized that, in my frustration, I had left without seeing all of the functions of the probe, and I resolved to dig deeper in our next meeting.

"Did you see the balls at the bottom of the probe?" he asked and I nodded. "That's how. Basically, we are going to drop from the orbital, we'll give them a little shove, and they will fall to the moon. While they fall, they will deploy an inflatable shell around them to protect them from the shock of the landing. Did you do that experiment in school where you had to protect an egg while it was being dropped from the roof? The one where whoever had the egg that survived would win? Well, my team and I always win that game." In the right circumstance Angelo's answer would have been funny, but in this case, it came across as arrogant and superior. "Once it lands safely on the ground, the lander uses a self-righting mechanism to orient itself for deflation. When it's positioned correctly, the air-filled safety bubble collapses. It sort of opens like a flower would open its petals to the sun, or if you like video games, it's like when Pac Man dies and his circle flattens out. You are left with an unfolded Wink Unit that's much bigger than you need to transport a person. Elegant and unique. Kind of our calling card"

It was like no sentence could leave Angelo's lips without rubbing me the wrong way. He had taken to calling me 'Vic," never Victor like I had asked him or even Chambers would be more acceptable. I had taken to calling him "Dick" in my head.

Riding the golf cart, we passed a variety of machining, storage, and assembly stations and made our way to the end of the building opposite where I entered. There was a gigantic bay door and right in front were the two additional rockets that would be used to escape Earth's atmosphere and then be discarded at the edge of space. They would peel off the main stage rocket like a banana skin. The booster rockets were noticeably similar to the main rocket, but distinctly smaller. Both looked intact and ready to go, but one had a slightly different nose cone than the other, it was longer and more pronounced and it was separated from the engine body of the rocket by what looked like an extra ring. There was an additional ring set by the second rocket, looking as though it still needed to be installed.

"What's that extra ring for?" I asked Angelo

"We need to add it to the other rocket to ensure both are evenly balanced in length and weight." He responded matter-of-factly.

"Sure, but it doesn't really seem to have much of a purpose. I mean the rocket looks whole without it and it doesn't seem to have anything in it. It's just extra mass, which I thought was a big no-no in space travel. The less weight the better." Something seemed off or at least it didn't make sense to my non-rocket-scientist brain. Angelo wasn't as glib as earlier conversations. He seemed more rushed.

"The rockets were just built at different times and we are trying to get them both evened up. Nothing special. Are you done here? I feel like I've given Uncle Sam more than enough of my time," Angelo said, waiving me to follow him back to the golf cart. I wanted to stick around and ask more questions, but didn't really have any questions rattling around my brain, and I realized I just wanted to waste more of Angelo's time.

On the drive back to the main gate, I was treated to a diatribe about the role of government in the lives of Americans and the businesses they own. According to Angelo, "We keep piling on regulations, and it's killing creativity. I have to employ an army of people just to cut red tape. Does that make sense? I should be able to launch a rocket when I want and where I want, within reason. I mean as long as I am not hurting anyone doing it. The risks I choose to take with my money and my life are my own." It was only a couple minute ride, but he used all of it to share his thoughts. He managed to cram in a night's worth of barroom conversation in the few remaining minutes we had, and it exhausted me. I was glad to leave.

I called Sara that night and filled her in. She pointed out that at least everything was on track for the launch, and it sounded like the specifications for the lander were followed well. Her Wink Pad would work well and the idea of redundancy seemed smart to her, though they hadn't intended to make a second Wink Unit and in particular a smaller one. She agreed to connect with Steve Angelo's people the next day to get the specs for the smaller craft and get her team working on the back up Unit. We stayed on and talked about Angelo's general ridiculousness. Sara chalked it up to the cost of genius, which I was sure Angelo would have relished. The conversation meandered until we were both too tired to talk anymore and we agreed to catch up again soon. I still hadn't worked up the nerve to make any kind of moves and was beginning to wonder if I ever would, like it was somehow out of my control.

The next visit to the Orbital Systems facility was just over a week later and about a week before the launch. The rockets were fully assembled and the Traveler was ready to be loaded, but Angelo didn't feel the need to meet me at the facility. Instead, I met with the government liaison officer. I was able to inspect the lander closely. Everything looked in order, though I wasn't able to see the Wink Unit in its final position as it wasn't ready to install at that time.

We met one more time as a task force, and I led the review and checklist for launch.

"Let's do one more run through of the checklist and make sure we are ready for next week." I said to the other three task force members. "Sara, is the Wink Unit assembly complete and ready to be loaded on the lander?"

"It is. The team tested a prototype of the lander and airbag deployment. Everything worked without an issue. I feel confident we will have a successful landing, assuming no problems with the launch, probe deployment, and navigation to the landing site." Sara seemed confident but exhausted. Everyone looked like they hadn't slept in the last week.

"That's a check for the lander. What about trajectory and systems?" I turned to Babu and asked.

"The calculations for the launch and landing are all complete and simulations confirm the launch timing. The trans-lunar injection model shows a perfect connection to the moon's sphere of influence and even allows for a convenient geostationary transfer orbit and the ability to drop the lander at Clavius Crater without Traveler needing to traverse an extra orbit to gain position. After we drop the lander, we will use the orbital's thrusters to gain a geosynchronous orbit and use Traveller as the command module for the lunar lander." Babu was as thorough and technocratic as always.

"Don't sound so excited." I said with thick sarcasm. We had a running joke on the team about Babu's deadpan delivery and infrequent joking. He was a serious guy and preferred talking about business. He gave an embarrassed smile at my comment and Sara and Simon giggled. We all secretly liked to make Dr. Gamal a little uncomfortable. It humanized his deep intellect and reminded me that he was likely the shy, but incredibly smart, kid at the back of class. "So, that is a check on the landing site and trajectory, how about systems and craft?"

"Check and check as well. I confirmed specs with orbital systems and we did the software load this week. Our JPL engineers did a smoke test as well and all systems were nominal." Simon confirmed.

"Excellent. I met with the folks at Orbital this week as well and all looked good, though it seems like Stan won't be making it to the big show. I was sort of looking forward to hearing the news casters making endless Stan jokes." I smiled thinking I was making a joke, but the audience didn't get it.

"Who is Stan?" Sara asked.

"The back up, smaller orbital." I said, assuming they didn't realize the orbital team had named it Stan.

"There were no plans for a backup orbital, and I never heard of a Stan." Simon added. "Maybe they were joking around with you. Did you hear about 'Stan' from Steve Angelo?"

"No, I saw it while I was at the facility. I asked Angelo why there were two, and he said redundancy. Seemed like a good answer." I was perplexed.

"Redundancy is a great idea. We just didn't have any plans for it given the short time frame. Angelo didn't say anything to me. That's a little odd." Simon said.

"Well, it better not end up on the bill after all his moaning about government overspending and conspicuous waste." I assumed we just had a miscommunication and it didn't seem like the long-lost Stan was hurting the mission any. "Traveler was ready and all areas seemed ready to go. I guess we don't need to worry about Stan."

"Agreed. I could use a drink and a meal. Anyone interested?" Sara said to the room, but she paused and looked directly at me.

"Definitely!" I said with too much enthusiasm.

"I'm in," added Simon and my heart sank just a little. Babu was out, which was pretty usual. I had developed a theory that he had a relatively severe case of social anxiety which made me even more interested in giving him the first giant hug I gave after our successful landing. The thought made me smile while we were having drinks.

Sara asked, "What are you smiling about?"

"I just had a thought about us landing on the moon successfully. That'll be a rush. Also, I was thinking about the moment we get confirmation the Wink Unit can receive an astronaut. I am sure we will be jumping around, and I am going straight for Babu and giving him the biggest hug I can." I smiled again, but bigger this time. Letting Sara into the conspiracy made it somehow more fun.

"Oh, he'll hate that! I'm in too." We both smiled at each other, I raised my glass and we toasted. The spark was definitely there. I should have asked her out then and there, but Simon was with us and things were going well. I didn't want to spoil it. All our boxes were checked. The team had a great dynamic. It was best not to look a gift horse in the mouth.

All that was left was the launch.

Victor Chambers (3)

A Moon Shot

Launch day came fast. The pieces all came together. The task force was in the control room of Orbital Systems in the Nevada desert. The room was a high-ceilinged semicircle with stadium style desks all facing toward the front of the room. An extremely large multi-panel display was prepared for the launch and was slowly ticking down the time until launch. A variety of people were at desks working on their part of the launch procedures. The whole operation was very professional which gave me a sense that the work everyone was doing was just part of their routine. Everyone had a job, and they seemed to know how to do it. To Angelo's credit, he seemed to know how to hire good people, and he let them do their jobs without a lot of interference. The task force observed the launch but did not actively participate. So, we were in the back of the room standing against the farthest wall and taking in the frenetic energy of the room.

Simon periodically worked the room, going from station to station and talking to the various controllers situated throughout the space. Things must have been going well since he was smiling the whole time. When the time came for the audible launch countdown to begin, Simon joined at the back of the room grinning from ear to ear and gave us a nod of approval.

"Everything looks good. This is by far my favorite part of the process." Simon said.

"Makes sense. Everyone loves to see the outcome of their hard work." I said in return.

"No. Not the launch. The time right before. I love the anticipation. The hope of all the people around the room. The anxiety and risk of such a big endeavor. Things in the room feel different. They smell different. Do you know what I mean?" Simon was clearly in his element and loving it.

"I think I do," I replied, getting a sense of the air around us.

"I certainly do," said Sara. "I have always loved the excitement before an event. The pressure builds up like a pressure vessel asking to be vented and only after the event takes place can anyone truly breathe freely." Her voice carried a sense of awe for the moment.

The chatter died down as the launch procedure entered its final moments. A voice came over the intercom, beginning the familiar countdown which culminated in him saying we have engine ignition. We all watched as a fire lit under the three engines of the rocket. The two boosters and the mainstage burned harder as the rocket lifted off the platform and headed for space. The rockets gained speed, and I got lost in the idea of how small the payload of the rocket was compared to the scale of the engines. It took so much work to get anything into space, but that would all change soon. We would have our extra-large Wink unit on the moon. The future of space travel would likely take place on the moon. Why launch from earth with gravity constantly trying to suck you back to earth when you could launch from the low gravity of the moon. To pull it off, you would just need to get all of the flight resources to the moon, but that wouldn't be a problem anymore. In fact, it would be easier than it used to be when we tried to move supplies around Earth. Expanding in the solar system seemed much less daunting as we could drop Wink stations on Mars or in orbit around Io. It wouldn't take a manned mission to get there, just dropping off the Wink unit and boom, humans are there.

I was snapped out of my thought spiral in time to hear them announce the booster stages were jettisoned and safely cleared the main rocket which was just entering its next stage of firing on the way to the moon. With the boosters falling slowly away back toward earth, everyone's attention was on the second stage of the main rocket while it ignited and sent Traveler hurtling towards the moon at around five miles per second.

The intercom announcer said, "We have a successful fire of the second stage rockets," and then there was a hubbub on the other side of the room. I heard engineers talking about booster rockets. Apparently one of the rockets had ignited again and sent the rocket back into space and off on an unknown trajectory. Simon and I walked over to the engineers to see what was going on.

"Hey, what's all the commotion about?" I asked.

A female engineer, clearly the one all the others deferred to, took up the thread and said, "It looks like there was some remaining fuel in the extra ring we added to one of the boosters. Luckily, it didn't ignite near the main rocket, or we might not be making it to the moon today. We were just talking about how that could have been missed by manufacturing, assembly, and the quality control processes."

"That is odd. How could fuel have leaked into the extra ring?" Simon asked, clearly flummoxed.

"I don't know, and we may never know. That rocket is long gone now." said the engineer.

"Well, I guess we can chalk it up to a lucky mishap and do a postmortem later. I really want to watch our package get delivered." I added, put my hand on Simon's shoulder and turned my head to the side in a gesture meant to bring Simon with me back to the main group for the remainder of the show.

We walked back to our unofficial station in the room and watched as the rocket continued its burn towards the moon. The trip to the moon would take a few more days and a couple hundred thousand more miles, but the launch phase was one of the most fraught parts of the trip and our craft had successfully made it. We shared a few moments of celebration in the room and all agreed to meet up for a few celebratory drinks later that day. Over the next two days, our focus would move to the space station that Babu Gamal was overseeing. We could turn our attention to the station since it was not necessary for us to track the rocket closely. We had regular updates coming through our phones. There wasn't much to see as the rocket traveled the distance between Earth and the moon.

The lunar base was a marvel unto itself as were the ever-expanding Wink pads. The pads were like a Russian nesting doll of tech, and on the last doll to be uncovered would be an entire moon base. The goal of the base was to wholly contain everything needed to support a team who would be traveling back and forth to the Moon daily. Wink tech had made it so a trip to the moon was a commute, taking only a couple seconds in transit. I had lost a night's sleep at one point thinking about where the astronaut was during the seconds, he was neither on Earth or on the Moon; While he was traversing the distance as energy or information rather than matter. I wasn't really sure where the in between was. In my mind, the traveler was nowhere at all.

Babu gave us a walkthrough of the base the first day. Walk through might be overstating it slightly since the space wasn't really large enough to walk around much, but it was plenty large to support the whole task force and a few others with about fifteen feet in diameter or just under two hundred square feet of usable space. It was basically a giant igloo of sorts. We launched a circular Wink pad and intended to use all the space possible, which meant a circular base. If you are aiming for a circle, you basically have igloo or yurt to work with. There were internal oxygen tanks to support a suit-off environment on the inside. When a tank got low, they could just Wink in a new tank. The concerns about sustainability had gone by the wayside, resupply was simple and planned.

The building concerns became more about utility and comfort. There were comfortable chairs but no beds since no one would need to sleep on the base. We could Wink in anyone and anything needed for experiments for a day if needed. The benches were made like Swiss army knives. They could support a variety of equipment and circled the exterior wall of the base. There were windows above the desks made of plate glass with a special coating. The creativity came out in the construction once weight was no longer a concern. The walls, where the plate glass wasn't present, had a liquid core to help protect against radiation. All-in-all the igloo was comfortable and safe.

The plan was to launch the first base, stabilize and test the platform and then launch others as quickly as possible. The individual igloo structures could be connected through above ground tunnels which connected at the entrances. Exits were not nearly as important. Realistically, people could just Wink from base to base, but humans need doors. Being in a room without an exit, even if there are windows, inevitably feels like being in a prison cell.

Within a few short months, if we did everything correctly, the surface of the moon would look a little like the complex on planet Spaceballs from the movie *Spaceballs*. Then the United States would claim as much land as we could for commercial development and start the building in earnest. Tourist traps would pop up and there would be new games, sports, and activities for the low gravity. At first visitors would need to be rich, but it wouldn't take long for that to subside considering the transportation costs would be zero. The only reason for the expense in the beginning would be the limited space available. I could see why President Sanderson wanted to claim as much land as we could, as quickly as possible. There were certainly other countries around the world doing the same. The space race was back on and we were in the lead.

The rest of the inspection was mostly about equipment and safety redundancies, which were interesting but not as sexy as the inner utility and the simplicity of the design. There were a few factors that had to be thought through in much more detail than a pop-up tent on Earth. Babu let us know about the special construction that was necessary due to the difference in temperatures on Earth versus the moon, expansion and contraction in the fastening was a real concern. If they didn't plan contraction as the base Winked from Earth to the Moon, the base would likely implode from strain. Also, the base would have to be tethered to the surface of the moon in some way to counterbalance the shifting that was possible due to the low gravity environment.

On the other hand, some things about building on the moon were easier. There was significantly less stress on the structural components of the building since there was far less gravity trying to pull the building down. Also, there was no need to weatherproof or earthquake proof the buildings. In the short term, the team would Wink fuel cells to the base to power everything, but the goal would be to build solar panels with battery packs to maintain the charge during the very long lunar nights. The team didn't really think existing solely off the moon would be either possible or necessary. The only reason to try to rely on lunar material for things like construction materials and oxygen extraction was because getting material to the moon was so expensive, no longer the case with the Wink tech.

The base build team did a practice run where they winked the entire moon base structure from one platform in the desert to another, which passed without incident. The process was captured on video which was fated to go viral after the base was delivered to the moon, until then it was confidential. The building being moved was incredible to watch since you could see both Wink pads at once. It made me think of a stage magic act in Las Vegas, "Watch as I make this entire Igloo disappear!" The only difference was you knew this was real. I guess that's true about technology in general. It's all sort of like magic, especially when it's new.

It seemed like everything was ready for the landing on the moon. We had to wait for Traveller to get to the moon and drop its payload still but all that could be done was done. The Russian-doll-Wink-units were ready, the astronauts were prepared to do the drop, the building was ready for deployment, and the rocket was on the way to the moon. It was a time where we could all go home, sleep a little and catch up on the parts of our lives that stayed in motion independently of the moon. There was a need to settle things before they became chaotic again.

Sleep didn't come easy with all the anticipation, but I did my best. I was up and down all night for the two nights that remained before the landing. I had a nagging feeling something was going to go wrong, but that was a feeling I had before most of the big days in my life. It kept me on my toes, though it was miserable while it was happening.

The morning of the landing was particularly rough for me. I woke up with a stiff neck, that feeling where you can't really turn your head and have to shift from the hips to look around. Rubbing my neck, I realized the problem seemed to start from my jaw. I must have been grinding my teeth all night. The dream I was having must have been intense. Though I didn't remember them when I woke up, I guessed they revolved around floating around in either the void of space or in the void between Wink units, probably the latter as I had those dreams before. A little coffee helped shake off the dream haze and a bit of Ibuprofen helped with my jaw and neck. Since I was already awake, I made my way to the control room early.

When I arrived at the control room there were a few people milling around and the overnight shift was just getting ready to head out. There was a bustle in the room, but the energy was less than would be present a few hours later when everyone would be eagerly tracking the progress of the lander as it headed to the surface. My goal was to stay back and observe, be a spectator, but one with a vested interest. There were a lot of things that could still go wrong. There could be issues with the orbital, issues with the lander, issues with the Wink unit, the astronauts could have problems, the base could fall apart. I was wishing we had built more redundancy into the lander and the Wink unit, taking a leaf out of Angelo's book.

As it turned out the orbital was positioned perfectly, which wasn't much of a surprise. Babu and Simon were amazingly competent, and they oversaw the process. We received confirmation that Traveler was in position to drop the lander and a countdown to drop began. When the launch director said "launch lander," the room collectively held its breath and waited for confirmation of a smooth release of the ball. Once the release was confirmed, everyone held their breath again while they waited for confirmation that the air sack bag had deployed. This time there was no confirmation. I heard a woman at a control say, "Repeat. That is negative deployment." There were a few moments of stunned silence, then from the back of the other side of the room we heard a voice say, "Deploy the second lander." It was Angelo. It reminded me that the days of NASA being in charge of launches was long past. It was up to private companies like Orbital Systems and Steve Angelo to manage the process. An affirmative response came from the control station and a second ball dropped to the Moon. This time we received a quick confirmation of the airbag deployment and a second confirmation of trajectory. We were slightly off course but not catastrophically so.

So, we all waited, again in silence, for confirmation of a successful bounce and landing. This was a longer wait, around ten minutes. The ball fell with little resistance but with less speed than it would have approached earth. It landed and the bounce was confirmed. I was told it bounced 1100 meters high. My mind spun out on what that might look like in a big city. It would have bounced three times higher than the Empire State Building. Looking at it from the ground, it would look like the ball shot right back up to the clouds, though it wouldn't reach them since clouds are generally about twice as high. Still, it would look tiny as it flew back up. The Burj Khalifa, on the other hand, is just short of the height of the bounce. So, if you were standing next to the Burj and the ball bounced next to you, you could watch as the ball bounced just past the tip of the building and came back down.

A couple bounces and a short roll later, the Wink unit was resting on the surface. The landing team called over Babu and shared satellite imaging of the landing site which was being sent by Traveller as it monitored the progress of the lander in its geosynchronous orbit. There was a concern the soil at the landing site was too unstable to support the Wink unit sitting upright. If there was a want to move locations, now was the time to do it as the lander was still in ball form. They were just getting ready to use the attitude adjustment motors to orient the Wink unit anyway. Babu confirmed they should adjust locations by a couple feet, and the team sent the instructions to the lander which, after a slight delay, we all got to watch on the big screen in the center of the room. Watching a giant ball start rolling without a push was a wonder on its own.

The locomotion mechanism was very clever. The air-filled ball was fitted with a series of openings around its surface which could release jets of air. When deflating permanently, and while in its final position, all of the openings would release air at the same time. To create motion, on the other hand, all they had to do was release air on one side and the ball would roll in the opposite direction. In the low gravity environment, it didn't take much to get the roll going.

Babu walked back to the group, and I asked, "Did we get a good parking spot?"

"Perfect," he answered. "The team here is really good." Babu smiled and looked satisfied but didn't add any additional words to the conversation as was his fashion.

The controller called for the deflation and the ball opened from the middle as designed. It split across its radius, starting at the top and slowly revealing the folded Wink Unit inside; opening like a clamshell. Once fully deflated, we were left with an image of a Wink unit sitting on top of a big yellow tarp, the deflated airbag. It looked perfectly poised to accept the first astronaut. The room broke out in applause. There was handshaking and a few hugs given around the room. The team and I all congratulated each other. I was saving my Babu hug for when we Winked the whole base. Spotting Angelo, I made my way across the room.

"Mr. Angelo," I called out to get his attention. He turned and acknowledged me and I could have sworn I saw his eyes roll.

"Mr. Chambers, are you here tracking your investment?" Angelo said with snark.

"I am." I said and smiled, trying to turn his comment into an inside joke. "Look, I just wanted to say congratulations and thank you for building that extra redundancy into the process. We wouldn't have a Wink unit on the moon right now if you hadn't. Well, I guess we would, but it would just be the one unsuccessful deployment scattered in pieces from the impact." I smiled again and reached out my hand.

Angelo reached out and shook it and said, "I told you we know what we are doing. We just need the freedom to do it. Maybe next time you guys can stay out of our way." Angelo smiled, but it was a wry smile and came as a companion to his barbed comments.

"Maybe we will. I am curious why you didn't mention the built-in redundancy on the craft? I mean I saw the other two balls on the craft, but I thought those housed other equipment." I couldn't understand his compulsive need to keep us out of the loop. In hindsight, it made sense that the matching balls on the body of the craft had the same purpose.

"You were right on one count. One of the balls houses the camera equipment but the other was obviously not a camera." Angelo responded, not answering the question.

"Well, I guess it's a good thing you are always ahead of us G-men." I said, giving Angelo one more big smile and reaching out my hand for a departing handshake.

"And I always will be." Angelo replied, gave my hand a quick shake and turned to engage someone else who he would clearly rather have been talking to.

The schedule called for a test of the Wink unit the night of the landing and, if all went well, the next day we would send our astronaut-delivery-man to drop off the larger Wink pad. In the best traditions of not wasting a trip to the moon, when the astronaut came back home to earth, he would bring back soil samples and use a ground penetrating radar to see what was below the surface. The next step would be another round of testing on the larger pad. The test for the mid-sized pad would consist of sending a vehicle, a lunar rover, to the planet so we can drive around. Provided there were no challenges in any of those stages, we would then launch the largest Wink Unit which would act as the foundation for the first ever base on the Moon.

Testing of the first Wink Unit on the moon went well. The control team decided to go simple, funny but symbolic with their test. And so, the first item to wink to the moon was a coffee cup with the saying, "Here men from the planet Earth first set coffee upon the moon" echoing the iconic plaque left during the first moon walk, of course with a slight twist. The cup made it to the moon and back. When it arrived at the facility the technician on duty picked it up and commented on how cold it was. The success of the test out of the way, we moved on to the first person to Wink to the moon.

The astronaut prepared by getting into the specially designed moon suit. It didn't look terribly different from the original suits worn by Neil Armstrong and Buzz Aldrin. The new suits had different coloring, the patches were more up to date, the material was thinner and lighter, but it had the same backpack that carried the oxygen supply which gave it the obvious air of a space suit. The gloves were thinner and more dexterous, which would help with the maneuvering of equipment and materials for the new moon base.

The astronaut approached the Wink pad hesitantly as if the pad itself was dangerous and not the act of transportation. He gingerly stepped on the pad. An assistant brought over the folded four-meter Wink unit which was shaped like a flower, like a rose before it opened to the sun with the petals swept to the side. It was just over two feet in diameter and around four feet tall. When it unfolded it was seven times larger in diameter. The spun-folded design made it easy to unfurl with just a single set of hands. The material was light enough the astronaut could easily hold the folder rig, though it looked a little ungainly in his arms.

The control director asked the astronaut, "Jim, are you ready to walk on the moon?" There was a hint of joy behind the serious words and Jim, the astronaut, replied with, "You better believe it."

The controller then said, "Good! We are a go for transportation. The Wink unit is powered up. Let's do this." The controller turned and gave a thumbs up to a technician who engaged the device and a moment later the astronaut and his cargo were gone.

Just a few moments later a clear voice cut through the silence of the room. We heard the intercom blurt, "Control, we are on the moon and it is beautiful. This is an amazing advance and offers the first concrete hope that humankind will finally live among the stars." The statement sounded a little rehearsed but that was likely because it was. It was an important moment and only a fool wouldn't have put some serious thought into what he would say with his first steps.

"Roger that, Jim. We're glad you're safe. You can proceed with the placement of the second Wink device. We are commencing with our transportation of the science kit and lunar safety equipment. Confirm once you have cleared the equipment from the Wink unit and we will send our next astronaut up to support you," said the control director.

"Copy that control. Can you confirm you're receiving my video signal as well?" Jim asked.

"Affirmative, Jim. We're receiving all signals from your suit including video and are in the process of bringing it up on screen and recording. We will confirm once we have visual," answered control.

They established the video connection moments later, and we were able to watch with surprising fidelity as Jim the astronaut removed the delivered equipment and began the procedures to unfold the second Wink pad. At the same time, a second astronaut named Hamari made her way through the Wink system to the lunar surface to assist Jim with the unfolding operations. The two astronauts positioned themselves on opposite sides of the folded "flower" and pulled near the base in opposing directions. The "flower" spun and unfolded at the same time until it laid flat on the ground, seven times larger in diameter than it had been. It was a perfect circle ready to receive its first passenger, the large lunar rover.

Unlike the original lunar rover, this vehicle was not an open-air convertible. Instead, it had an enclosed cabin which was pressurized and provided with enough oxygen to last fifteen hours. It was a secondary moon base in a lot of ways. Loaded on the pad on earth, it was winked to the moon with no incident. The two astronauts entered the vehicle, did a systems check and then called for the final Wink Unit to be sent, the one large enough to support the full-sized Moon base. It arrived on the four-meter pad and looked too small to be the resting place of a moon base as it was only a little over six feet in diameter, though it was nearly twice as tall. Still, the materials used to make the Wink

Unit were very light. I could easily lift the mid-sized Unit on earth. With the lower gravity on the moon, the two astronauts had no trouble removing the large Wink Pad and getting it into position.

Earth-side, the moon base was prepared to wink to the moon. The team had done the final systems check and ran through the checklist of items that were expected to be present on the base, important items like the oxygen tanks. The countdown to the first lunar base was underway and the room was quiet with anticipation. I think the launch was such a big deal since it really was the first thing we were doing as a team that was totally new. Humans had launched a rocket to the moon, walked on it, driven on it, but had never taken up residence. We were about to leave our mark for all time.

"Confirmation. The base was successfully transported," said the control director over the intercom system. "Moon team, can you confirm visual on the base?"

"Confirmed. We have a base on the moon!" said Hamari. The excitement was clear in her voice. The team at the control center went wild. There was a din of noise that shook the ceiling tiles. For a few minutes it was like the encore at a rock and roll concert. Sara and I locked eyes, both smiled and immediately grabbed hold of Babu and hugged him. He wiggled in our arms but we weren't going to let go. We started hopping up and down and Babu had to follow suit. To make it worse, Sara kissed him on the cheek. All our energy was spent on the excitement, we stopped jumping but Sara and I were still holding each other's arms. Finally, Babu said, "Please let me go," in his deadpan manner, not angry, just ready to be on his own. We obliged quickly but there was emptiness as everyone else was still celebrating. I looked at Sara, held out my arms, and smiled. She smiled back and stepped into my arms, wrapping her arms around my back.

It was bliss. I found my courage and asked, "Any chance you would want to go to dinner with me?" What I had done hit me and I immediately felt my face redden. I cleared my throat which seemed to collapse under the pressure. "Ehrm, just me that is. Just the two of us?"

"I was just going to ask you the same question," Sara said with the hint of mischief in her voice.

Victor Chambers (4)

Live Among the Stars

The excitement following the landing on the moon was feverous. The news media was everywhere, and there were celebrations nearly every night for a couple weeks. Sanderson's approval ratings were at record highs, and it felt like America was back on top. There were other nations heading to the moon, but they decided to approach things differently. The European Union opted to land a Wink pad and send building materials to the moon, building on the surface, which was labor intensive and required temporary shelters. The Chinese sent robots to do the work. We were up and running first and as a result were able to stake our claim to a larger area of land with the best resources available.

Eventually, the other space-faring countries matched our technique. It was obvious our design was the clear winner. The American base became known as Khonshu in honor of the orbital. About a month after we set up the base, we sent a science mission to explore the area around the base for resources. A team of four scientists were taking soil samples and digging into the bedrock, three in the base and one on a moon walk to drill for a deeper core sample when the control base back in Nevada received a warning. The alarms were going off and the computers were registering a loss of air pressure. The moon is pockmarked with craters from meteor and asteroid impacts and there was still plenty of debris floating around our solar system. Generally, the debris doesn't impact the ground of Earth very often since the atmosphere acts as a barrier but with the barely existent atmosphere of the moon, things hit periodically. The control team assumed a small impact had punctured the walls of Khonshu base and hit the failsafe button. The entire base was transported back to Earth in two seconds.

It turned out to be a false alarm. One of the monitors was faulty. The control team should have checked the other monitors to confirm the pressure loss, but they were a little too excited and brought the whole base home. The bad news was there was still a scientist outside the base and a few moments after the Khonsu was winked home a voice was heard over the communications system that said, "Um, Nevada base, this is Alestor. I just made it back to Khonshu base, and the base isn't here. Please advise." Media outlets were listening when the voice came over the speaker and the mishap went viral nearly instantly. The story made for a great Saturday Night Live sketch, a few great magazine cartoons, and wonderful fodder for the late-night talk shows. It also showed how easily our system could save astronauts who were in distress. The world laughed, but they also hopped on the bandwagon as quickly as possible.

In no time at all, the moon was getting populated. Sandals Resorts signed the first corporate deal to build on the moon. They built a large resort with a built-in amusement park. With low-gravity the rides were much more interesting. Large bungee jumps, giant drops and sharper turns on rollercoasters. It became one of the most popular vacation locations for years, with the surprise attraction being the swimming pool. Sara and I visited the resort prior to the opening day, and there was no doubt that swimming in low-gravity was a singular experience. I particularly liked diving off the diving board. I was able to get a giant spring and do flips while landing relatively gently in the water, hitting the water in the pool was incredibly forgiving. A belly flop wasn't a big deal at all. You could also jump like a dolphin out of the pool and actually fully exit the water. The only problem is that splashes and waves in the pool tend to get a bit out of control. A cannon ball into the pool resulted in a surprisingly big wave which would slosh around as it settled over a protracted period of time. I guess one could say we had conquered the moon when humanity started serving corn dogs and Moon-themed soda cups with crazy straws.

Once humanity had settled on the moon, it was time to move on to bigger and better things. I took a post with NASA as part of their mission planning team. My experience with the Khonshu mission was valuable, and the plan was to move on to Mars as quickly as possible. The nations of the world were battling to claim the next prize which seemed, logically, to be Mars though there were some who disagreed and were sending spacecraft to Jovian moons and the like. America has had a love affair with Mars for a long time and public sentiment was behind a big push to Mars. Leaving the solar system, while attractive conceptually, was still a bit out of the question. The rough math said it would take around five years to wink to Alpha Centauri, which on its own sounded terrifying considering during the trip the traveler would be nowhere, but also it would take thousands of years to deliver the Wink unit. So, we were stuck in our home solar system.

Mars is between three and twenty-three light minutes from Earth, depending on the relative positions in solar orbit, which meant the travel between Earth and Mars was reasonable for Winking, but getting the Wink Pad to Mars would take time. The plan called for approximately six months to build and another six months to travel. We had a year to plan. In the meantime, we were doing our best to work out a landing location. The goal was to find the right combination of resource availability and geographic stability. The tools to find the location were close at hand since America launched a variety of missions which left behind usable rovers and probes. The rovers were set to finding a suitable location. The clearest need was for a stable location, resources became secondary as we could Wink most anything needed on the surface from Earth. Long term, resources would matter, but with the small expeditions that would get us started resources were much less important.

There were a dozen probes on Mars all sent at different times, some newer and others limping along. Pathfinder, Viking, and Opportunity were all near each other as we were preparing for our mission and the others were more evenly spread across the planet. We had a few suitable locations already pinned, but we were hoping to find an area where water ice was more abundant. We had time to do so while the building and planning were underway. So, we rovered around the planet and used satellite images to get a picture of our location. We learned a few things from our year plus on the moon and the work that led to colonization. We realized that perfection wasn't necessary, but there would be competition for resources like water. There was another rush to stake a claim just like on the Moon. This time the challenge was a little more complex since we weren't the only group who had learned from the moon work and there was a good chance our model of modular colonization via giant Wink unit would likely be copied. Speed became the order of the day. The trouble was we were only counting on foreign nation competition which ended up being a big mistake.

About fourteen months after our moon base first landed, I was woken up in the middle of the night by a call from the Mars control station which was still based in Houston, Texas. I was living in a suburb named Friendswood, which was close to the mission control center but still provided some distance and a fair amount of greenery. I opted to rent a house while I was there since I figured I would be staying in the area for at least a couple years. I wanted a place that was nice enough Sara would want to come visit and not just come into town because I was there. Friendswood fit the bill nicely.

The call came with a panicky voice. "Mr. Chambers, we think we found something."

"It's pretty early, or is it late? Erhm, it's really both. Couldn't it wait until tomorrow?" I stammered.

"I don't think so. You better get down here as fast as you can." The woman on the other end of the call was named Linda. She wasn't the type to play a joke and wasn't prone to unnecessary alarm. I knew I needed to rouse myself.

"Copy that. I'm on my way." I perked up as much as I could, slapping myself in the face with some water from the bathroom sink, used a little mouthwash, and threw on the first clothes my hands rested on in the closet. I was out the door and in my car in less than five minutes, opting to aid winking in case that was at the root of the concern. The drive was about twenty minutes with no traffic, which was rare since the adoption of winking. That day I made it in under fifteen aided by the complete lack of cars on the road and a disregard for the police. My mind was racing with the possibilities. What could have caused them to get me out of bed at that hour?

When I arrived at mission control, there was a group of people huddled in the middle of the room looking at a monitor and talking animatedly. They clearly hadn't noticed me and were unlikely to disengage from their conversation and whatever was on the screen. I walked over to the group, looked at the screen and said, "What am I looking at?"

The group collectively jumped and Linda squeaked. She quickly said, "Oh good, you're here. Look at this. That's the Curiosity rover. It bumped into that." Linda pointed at the screen at what looked like a black rock outcropping.

"That bit of rock? Isn't that a pretty normal occurrence? I mean it's not like we have real time remote control." I answered, honestly perplexed.

"That's not rock, or at least rock like that shouldn't exist on Mars." Linda said.

Looking closer the edges seemed a little sharp to be natural and the angles were off too. The camera feed on Curiosity was low resolution and after bumping into whatever the black structure was, the camera was too zoomed in to be able to take stock of the object in detail.

"Can we back up and get a good look?" I asked.

"Nope. We are stuck. It must have lodged a wheel when it collided with that thing." Linda said.

"Well, what are we thinking?" I asked the group.

"Here are our rough options. It could be another craft from another nation that somehow got off course, but it seems too big for that. It's possible it could be something like obsidian or another black volcanic rock but we haven't seen anything like it before. Or, it could be that other option," Linda said sheepishly.

"What other option?" I asked, laughing with mild frustration.

"Other life. Marvin Martian. You know. That." Linda was clearly discounting the final option. She had that air of Occam's razor cutting it a little too close for comfort.

"What does the rest of the group think?" I asked the broader audience and the group erupted in chatter. They shared theories and heckled each other over which idea had the most merit. After a few moments I said, "Okay, I get it. Everyone is excited. Me too. What do we do next?"

"We hold out for the higher resolution images, and then start making some plans," Linda said.

In about an hour we had higher resolution pictures and it showed an all-black, domed structure. The dome had a Buckminster Fuller look about it, looking like the classic Bucky Ball design that was so popular in the mid-eighteenth century. My initial reaction was that it had to be man-made. Then I started to think it might not be man-made, but maybe made by intelligent life of the non-human variety.

"That's a structure," I said.

"It sure is," said one of the scientists. He was caught in the moment and had awe in his voice, not condescension.

"Is it alien?" I asked. "How could we miss this in our satellites?"

"Well, only around ninety percent of Mars is mapped with high resolution images. The structure is big, but it isn't big enough to really register as much on the low-resolution images. Also, we don't take new pictures constantly. It could have just been missed," Linda answered.

"That's crazy! Are we really seeing the first sign of Martians?" I said, incredulous.

"Maybe, but it really looks human. Is there something happening in other countries that we don't know about? Chambers, that's your area, right?" Linda asked me, but addressing the crowd. She wasn't accusing, but hopeful I might have some information.

"Not that I know of. I think we are at the tip of this spear. We are the closest to getting to Mars based on our conversations with other countries and the intelligence reports," I said. "Maybe it is actually alien? Could that be possible?"

"Sure, anything is possible. God, that would be amazing. What if it is alien?" One of the assembled scientists added enthusiastically. I noticed right then and there the idea could take hold quickly and likely spread.

"First order of business is a more thorough examination. We need a better understanding of what we are looking at before we communicate this externally." My cautious side was on display.

It wasn't long before the team found something that changed the whole picture, and the world. Linda approached me with a slightly grainy print out of the side of the Martian structure on one page and a print of an image from the internet on a second page.

"Look at this. This is what we are seeing." Linda said clearly, incredulously.

"Holy shit! That's the Orbital Systems logo, isn't it?" I was stunned, jaw on the floor. She was right. The grainy image from the Martian structure had a printed picture of a sphere with a ring around it, the ring turning into a rocket as it passed a planet. It was Orbital Systems. But how in the world could it be Angelo and his company? We monitored all launches, and he didn't have one headed for Mars, much less one that could have been launched long enough ago to allow them to be built on Mars already. I had one option in front of me and that was a direct conversation with Angelo, along with a series of notifications to the political and intelligence arms of the United States government.

I notified the appropriate agency and asked for a meeting with Angelo. "Asked for" was probably not a perfect representation of my approach. I demanded to talk with him. Even as a demand, Angelo managed to delay me for a few days by saying he was very busy. Given what we found, I was sure he was busy. In the time between our discovery and my meeting with Angelo, a lot of questions needed to be answered. Was what Angelo and his company did legal? The short answer seemed to be yes. As Orbital Systems was a U.S. based company, was the Mars base seizeable by the United States government?

Perhaps was the answer we received from our legal team. They were quick to point out how nothing like this had ever been adjudicated in court and the closest we may get is a claim of eminent domain, though that could be a stretch. The biggest question was, who did the land claimed by Angelo and Orbital Systems belong to? Was it U.S. property, Earth property, or was it all Angelo's? Could he create his own independent state? A tricky question for sure and the lawyers didn't have an answer. It seemed like the Martian base could be Angelo's sovereign land and the longer he had unfettered access to Mars, the more land he could claim. He could build the independent state of Steve Angelo.

I managed to schedule a meeting with Angelo a week after our bumping into each other on Mars. I guessed that he had observational equipment on his end and noticed our rover sniffing around. He was likely as interested in talking as I was. I could imagine the childlike eagerness that likely possessed him in knowing that he had got one over on the government. So, I had to prepare before I could confront him, which I looked forward to for the catharsis.

We met at a coffee shop outside Las Vegas. There were only a few tables in the whole place and only one other table was occupied which gave a sense of clandestine solitude to an issue that already had a feeling of spy craft. Angelo was sitting, staring at his cell phone with a steaming coffee cup in front of him. It was obvious he hadn't drunk any yet since there was still a heart shaped pattern in the foam of his drink. He seemed singularly occupied by his phone and didn't really notice me as I walked up.

"Mr. Angelo." I said curtly as I grabbed the back of the chair across from Angelo to sit down.

"Vic. How are you?" Angelo asked without a hint of sincerity.

"Honestly, I'm a bit confused. I am hoping you can shed some light on things for me." I answered.

Angelo set his phone down next to his coffee cup, rested his elbows on the table and steepled his fingers tips. "I bet you are. So, why don't you fill me in on what's got you out of sorts today."

A nice subtle insult to start the exchange, I resigned myself to a conversation that was unlikely to be pleasant. I said, "I think you probably know, but let me lay it out for you. One of our Mars rovers bumped into something while on a scouting mission. It was big, domelike and had an Orbital Systems logo on it. I don't recall any authorized missions to Mars for Orbital Systems, and I am unaware of any equipment your company built for our missions. So, I am confused how something from your company ended up on Mars."

"I could see how that could cause confusion. I mean after all; NASA has conducted a series of missions to Mars but never really set up an effective way to monitor the whole surface. Things could be happening all over Mars and you would have no idea. That would lead to a perpetual state of confusion. Though I bet your question isn't really about how you didn't notice, but how did *we* get there before you?" Angelo asked.

"Fine. That." I said frankly.

"Well, really I should say thank you for that." added Angelo. "We weren't likely to get an easy clearance to send a probe to Mars, but you and your team provided me with the perfect opportunity. If you had known a little more about rocket design, you might have figured it out, though I admit I thought you were close at one point. You see, the booster rocket that 'blew up' during the Khonshu launch didn't really blow up. It operated as designed. It launched a secondary rocket sending a probe to Mars. Not a big probe but it didn't need to be big. Only big enough to land a Wink pad on Mars so we could get the rest of our equipment there. Actually, I should thank you a few times. Your Moon launch got us there. Your design for foldable Wink units and a base on a Wink pad were all wonderful tools in our tool chest. We were perfectly positioned considering we had the inside view of everything you were planning and helped your build and launch. We copied a fair amount of your designs, if I am being honest."

"If I am being honest, that feels a bit like treason. Don't you think?" I was pissed and let it show.

Angelo was unfazed. "I guess it is, if you assume that somehow the United States government owns Mars, but it doesn't. Trust me, over the last ten months or so our lawyers have checked every possible claim, and they assure me Mars is mine. Well, ours, I guess. We do have shareholders." Angelo ended with another one of his signature wry smiles, picked up his coffee cup and sipped for the first time and much louder than was absolutely necessary.

"What now? I mean you carved out your own little country on another planet. What does someone who hates government do when he has to build one?" I wanted to point out his hypocrisy, since he didn't seem to see it.

"Government isn't really the problem. It has its purpose. Someone has to coordinate things to make the trains run on time. I think about it like my business. Orbital Systems needs executives and managers. We need people in HR to make sure we don't act overly stupid. We need people to do all of the jobs that keep us in business. Some of what we do is infrastructure and some of it aspirational, but it all strives for a purpose. A goal set by the leadership, the board…me. I pay people to help me accomplish that goal. The government isn't all that different. The problem I have with the government is that it tries to go beyond its scope way too often. Some politician gets a wild hair that it is wrong to do something, and it tries to step in and tell me I can't, even when it isn't in service of the goals of the country or the leaders who are guiding. I know how to stay out of people's way. OS will set things up on Mars so we don't try to infringe on people in their free time. Less rules, less government, more freedom, more liberty." Angelo answered. The logic wasn't lost on me, but it was too simplistic.

"And what happens when one person in your little city decides to steal from another or worse? Government has to get in people's way. You don't know what it means to do the business of governing. You have to make rules. If you don't, the people will take over and make their own. Safety and security, prosperity and harmony require structure. They don't arise out of anarchy. Once a government starts making rules, it's really hard to stop. You'll fall into that trap too, even if you think you are above it. I just hope you don't hurt people learning your lessons in governing." I was offended. I reflected on it later and realized Angelo's perspective cut me a little deeper than I recognized at the time. His anti-establishment bullshit was a judgment on how I had spent my life. I worked in the service of my country for too many years to hear that what I was doing didn't have value. Also, Angelo was a dick about it. The combination gave me a strong dislike for him.

My conversation with Angelo was done, and I left him like I found him. His head buried in his cell phone and his coffee not being touched, just there as a prop to allow him his smug punctuation in our conversation. I imagined him leaning back in his chair after I was out of sight, satisfied with another Angelo accomplishment.

That was how control of Mars, or at least a huge portion of Mars was claimed by what would become one of the largest companies in the solar system. Within a few days Angelo went public and shared with the world what he had already built. There was a whole infrastructure up there. He was right, his team moved faster than we could. They had already built separate modules for science, tourism, waste management, energy production, and executive offices for his team. It was a multi-unit complex that he intended to grow. He even sent up one of his tunnel boring machines to make passages underground to connect his bases. We had to admit he won.

To make matters worse, the Orbital Systems team already started the process of making a variety of alliances around the globe. They signed a contract to help with additional construction and had a plan to use the Martian soil that was excavated during their tunneling to build bricks that would be used to make new structures. Even though materials could be sent from Earth, there was a novelty in using native Martian material to build. OS signed a deal with the European Union, who were in on the launch relatively early but wouldn't admit how early, to have the first embassy on Mars. The rumor was Angelo promised the EU land on the planet so they could build a larger outpost, but they had to agree to stipulations. Given Angelo's distaste for government I imagined it had to do with recognizing his land as an independent nation with a right to self-rule and likely a relatively lucrative agreement to use the Orbital Systems for their supply and Martian infrastructure needs.

The American mission to Mars was quickly scrapped. Waiting eighteen months to get there and build was mostly out of the question since the locations where we most wanted to build would likely be taken by then. We met as a team and couldn't find a better way forward. We signed a contract with OS for our Martian habitation project. I couldn't bring myself to participate in the negotiations and abdicated my part in the process. Orbital Systems had become the first company to also be a nation, its board was the first fully formed and functioning corporatocracy. The structure turned out to be oddly successful. OS opened huge revenue streams headed by Angelo; they built like children with Legos. Every structure was unique, they weren't constrained the way a democratic government might be since they didn't have a population to please, only employees to retain and shareholders to satisfy. With their semi-monopoly on Mars and the income they collected from it, OS had no resource restrictions.

The OS team named their Martian town Orbital City which felt a little like naming it Disneyland to me, but it caught on and began to sound normal in the way that most names do when used enough. Looking back at my career, it's easy to say I was part of something big but I also can't help feeling like a lot of my story is really just the story of Steve Angelo from another perspective. I was lucky enough to go along for the ride. I never did like him. We had plenty of reasons and opportunities to interact over the coming years as we both participated in the colonization of Mars, but our philosophies never lined up. I guess you don't have to like someone to respect them and he was certainly deserving of respect. Afterall, a person can't accomplish everything he accomplished and not at least earn a little awe.

Justin Skay (1)

A New Hope

It's not like I loved where I grew up or anything. That's not the right way to say it. I knew I didn't want to stay there, not because it was a bad place to live, just that it was small. You know what I mean by small. There wasn't much to do. I already knew everyone and had done everything there was to do. The people were okay and it was pretty and all, but maybe it never really felt like home. My hometown felt more like a place to be from, not a place to be. My plan was to leave after high school. I didn't. I stuck around like most everyone else who was from Unalaska, Alaska.

I worked at the Safeway bagging groceries and eventually worked the registers. They weren't bad days. I look back on it now, and I think it might have been smarter to stick around. Unalaska is beautiful in the summer and pretty in the winter too, if you like snow. There weren't many girls to get to know, but I guess there weren't many boys for the girls either and things balanced out. I dated a girl from high school. She was a sophomore named Julie Tucker. She was cute and came from an outdoorsy family. There were a lot of families like that in Unalaska. I guess that's why people wanted to live there. There was fishing, hunting, skiing, hiking, and no end to pretty things to look at. The harbor was cool, the mountains were pretty and there was wilderness for days.

My family wasn't the outdoorsy type. My dad worked on the fishing boats and mom left when we were pretty young. So, it was just my sister Janine and I taking care of ourselves. We would pretty much just stay at home and watch TV or hangout with some of the kids from nearby houses. Julie said that I was a "homebody" and tried to get me to go out on hikes and stuff with her. I did a couple times, but didn't really see the appeal.

Julie left after high school. She was younger than me. I had a girlfriend in town until I was twenty, but then it was just me and my dad for the most part. Janine had left for college. She was smart and growing up the way we did made her independent and comfortable to leave home right at eighteen. Janine was two years older than me and dad was out on the boat a lot, which left me with the house all to myself for a lot of my last two years of high school. At first, having the place to myself was pretty cool. I had people over; we were able to drink and stay up all night. Eventually though, it started to feel lonely, especially after high school when a lot of my friends started leaving for the Lower Forty-Eight.

Wink tech changed things. Not right away. We heard the news about the leak. It was a topic of conversation around town, but there wasn't any concern about it impacting our backwater islands up north. The news channels talked about drug running and terrorism in the early days which made the tech seem more like a problem our little town wouldn't have to deal with. Things really shifted when President Sanderson was elected and the tech was given the thumbs up by the government. Things shifted even more when stores started selling Wink units at surprisingly affordable prices. A couple of the local hotels and restaurants added Wink pads and people who couldn't normally visit started showing up for a peek at the town.

We were getting a few dozen new visitors each day. My manager at the Safeway told me sales had gone way up. He seemed pretty excited by the influx of new people. Most people were excited in the beginning. The number of people visiting wasn't overwhelming. It reminded folks of when one of the boats from Dutch Harbor was part of a reality TV show. It brought in some new business and put our name on the map. The peace was sort of doomed.

Things got out of hand when a social media influencer winked in for a day trip and posted a high-pitched endorsement of our "pretty little town." She came in the summer and managed to catch a couple of amazing days. The place looked like something out of a Hobbit movie and the internet blew up.

Soon, there were hundreds and then thousands of new visitors coming every day. The city had decided early, when there were only a few dozen people coming every day, to add a bunch of Wink stations by the World War II memorial which was already by the airport and seemed like a smart place to get people started on the island. The stations were open, with no limitations on how many people could travel into town. So, people would just wink in all day. It was crazy. You couldn't even go to Town Park, the park near my house, because it was overrun by kids from all over the world, speaking languages I hadn't even heard. It got so bad there was even a day I had trouble getting home through all the foot traffic.

Keep in mind Unalaska only had like five thousand people to start with, and it's not like there was a ton of land where people could just spread out. There are hills and stuff outside of the town, but the town itself is small. It couldn't handle the population doubling overnight. The hotel capacity wasn't really the issue since people would just wink home every night. It was the sheer number of people coming to town. They overwhelmed everything.

I went to meet some friends at the Norwegian Rat Saloon, which was pretty close to where I worked, and I couldn't even get in the door. It was crazy noisy too. I saw one of the waitresses I knew from high school. She looked like she had just run a marathon. I waved to her over the crowd of people standing shoulder to shoulder in front of me and yelled her name, but I couldn't get through the noise and density of the crowd.

The whole town started to get messy. There was trash all over the place that had been brought from wherever the visitors came from and left on our streets. Unalaska doesn't really have trees on the hills around it either. There is mostly grass, very green grass in the summertime, but not a lot of trees. People were climbing up and down the hills to get a better view which made the hills look like they were ant hills crawling with bugs. The traffic robbed the area of what natural beauty it had.

The mess of people everywhere made me feel even more lonely. There was something incredibly depressing about having all those people around and still not having a girlfriend or many friends and going home to an empty house every night. I was feeling down when I went to work one day. My manager asked me what was wrong. He told me something that's stuck with me. He said, "Sometimes you never feel more alone than when you're with people." He was right.

I was up one night, messing around on my phone way too late. I couldn't really sleep because there was a ton of noise outside my window, near the park. It was one of those nights where the smallest sounds would keep me awake. I was playing a mindless game on my phone, getting blocks to stack up just right, and an ad for a new app called Bramble came up. There was a picture of the world and the scrolling text said, "With Wink you can be anywhere." The map zoomed in and out of recognizable locations around the world and it showed couples eating and at the beach, climbing mountains and getting coffee. Of course, everyone looked incredibly happy. Then the ad said, "You can be anywhere, and you can go on a date anywhere. Join Bramble and scour the globe looking for your future partner." It zoomed back out to a spinning globe.

Online dating or app dating, or whatever people called it, wasn't really in my wheelhouse. People lie about themselves. They make themselves out to be more than they were in reality, better looking, more interesting, more successful or at least that's what I heard. Besides, what in the world do you do with a dating app when you live on a tiny island in the middle of the Bering Sea? I mean, I knew everyone who I could possibly meet. It was late, my judgment was impaired, and I made a profile. The app said they could match me with anyone in the world. It wanted to know my preferences down to the littlest detail. I guess with that many options, you need a lot of details to narrow down the field. I chose a ton of the criteria at random but there was a choice group where my preferences were for good reasons. There were questions that seemed pretty reasonable like, "How do you feel about dogs?", but others that seemed really odd like, "If you could live to one hundred years old would you rather your mind or your body work?" and "Is cereal soup?" I made sure to select English speaking girls who were into watching TV figuring that was my main genre. I hit submit at the end and tried to forget what I had just done since I felt a little ashamed.

I checked back in the morning and the dating app had found hundreds of potential matches. There was an English girl whose profile said she just finished college, moved back home and was looking for someone to "watch Baywatch with in Germany." I guess she had a Hasselhoff fetish. There were a few American girls, but since I took the plunge already, I decided to go with someone from a culture that was less familiar. A girl named Nari from Korea said she liked sitcoms, and pizza which sounded about right and I clicked to save her profile. I saved another from a Futurama fan from Belgium, though I think I might have been more interested in waffles since it was early, and I was hungry. By the way, I know there is more to Belgium than waffles but the brain sorta does what it wants sometimes. When I was done scrolling, I had around a dozen girls I was going to message. It would have been hard for me to admit this at the time, but the whole process was pretty exciting. It's easier to accept the idea as I get older. I realize now I was looking for an adventure and the app was a way to get started. It turned out to be an adventure I didn't expect and really didn't want. Like Bilbo said, "You step onto the road, and if you don't keep your feet, there's no knowing where you might be swept off to."

My first date from the Bramble app was sort of a disaster. We matched based on what seemed to be a love for Bond films. I didn't see much else in her profile that would link us together. Playing to the theme, we set a date in Thailand at those really cool islands from *The Man with the Golden Gun*. They apparently call it James Bond Island for westerners, but in Thai it's called Ko Khao Phing Kan. The island is super tropical and there is a bay called Phang Nga that has, what look like, plant covered statues in the middle of the bay that sort of defy gravity. The tour photos showed the option to go into the caves from the Bond film, visit the bay and beach, and get boated around the island. The whole trip was supposed to take about eight hours, which in hindsight is far too long for a first date but the Wink Tech was new and the options for dates were kind of unlimited, and I didn't know better. Lesson learned.

The Wink site closest to our departure point was at a resort. The resorts were stocking up on Wink Units because people weren't feeling the need to stay at hotels nearly as much. They hoped to cash in on the Wink travelers by getting them into their restaurants or other amenities. The resort put the Wink Unit in the middle of hotel amenities. When I winked in, I was next to the main restaurant, the spa, and a really large pool. It was a really nice hotel and nothing like being in Unalaska. It was tropical like watching Hawaii 5.0 or Magnum PI (I know, that's Hawaii). There were cool little huts and palm trees everywhere.

I arrived about thirty minutes early and used the time to wander around. I expected to see more people but there weren't many at the resort. Oddly, there were less people wandering around than were invading my home town. The ocean water was a much lighter blue. I dipped a toe in and the warmth of the water surprised me.

Yana showed up a little late. I was waiting for her at the Wink station for about fifteen minutes when she winked in, matching the picture from her Bramble profile. She was prettier than I expected. I saw face shots, but after taking her in I would have guessed she was a model which would have been a big score for me, though I had a feeling right from the second she saw me that it wasn't going to work. We locked eyes almost immediately, and she looked instantly disappointed. I introduced myself, she gave me a curt hello and checked her cell phone for something, maybe she sent a text or maybe she was checking my picture on Bramble to make sure her disappointment was warranted.

She was from Kharkiv, Ukraine but could have easily been from any high school cheerleading squad in any "mean girls" type movie. Her accent was

Russian sounding, but I thought I caught a touch of…like…Valley Girl in there. Figuring small talk may help, I tried to crack a joke.

"Kind of cool that we can meet in Thailand. Sort of surreal. I mean five years ago I wouldn't have guessed I would ever be able to afford a trip anywhere like Phuket." I intentionally mispronounced Phuket and gave a peevish smile to see if I could get a reaction and maybe get rid of the look on her face that made it seem like she had just smelled something awful.

I got no smile. She just said, "It's pronounced poo-ket. Not fuck it," she rolled her eyes and looked back at her phone. Checking the time maybe?

"So, you're into Bond films?" I asked, giving it another try.

"Not really. I just put that on my page as a joke. My dad is into that stuff. He's the head of a software engineering company. He's kind of a botanik. You know, a "nerd." Yana said with extra emphasis at the end to show how pedestrian the word was and to highlight what a botanik I must also have been for liking the same stuff. I had eight more hours with her where she was either unimpressed or totally disinterested. It was a long day, and at the end, I decided I would have to go back to James Bond Island with someone who was more of a botanik, like me.

My second date wasn't much better, but for different reasons. After the failure of the first, I decided on a plan that was a little more tried and true, just coffee. I figured if I was going to do coffee, I should try a place that was known for coffee. A quick google search later and a filter on my Bramble matches for coffee lovers and I was setting up a date with a girl from Australia at a coffee shop in Havana, Cuba. The coffee shop had a set of Wink units and had been pretty popular. Thinking ahead, I booked a reservation. I figured in the worst-case scenario I would get to see a little of Cuba and have a cup of coffee or two, no big-time commitment, and it cost way less.

My date's name was Amelia and she was from Sydney. She had dark hair and vaguely Asian features. Her profile said she was a coffee lover and had just finished re-watching Game of Thrones for the third time. She was right on time and met me with a smile. She even introduced herself. I love Australian accents and Amelia's was awesome right from the word "hello." While we waited in line to order, we chatted about how cool it was that we could meet in Cuba. The cafe seating was full by the time we got our drinks, even though we had made reservations. We laughed about it and took our coffee to go and decided to walk around the city. I wasn't really worried about getting lost, figuring we could use the maps app on my phone to find our way back.

Our conversation was awesome. I found out that a big part of her family was of Chinese descent having moved to Australia like a hundred years before. She talked about feeling a little on the outside in school because of her heritage and that she used TV and movies as an escape into other people's lives. I related but for a different reason. In Unalaska, there wasn't a ton to do if you weren't into the outdoorsy stuff, which I wasn't. Movies and TV were my way of getting out of town and "meeting" people who were more like me.

The date was going great and Havana was beautiful. There were people all around us and classic cars from the 50s and 60s drove by the whole time. We walked around a little park that had a big classic looking church on one side, and buildings that looked like housing surrounding the other sides, many of which were being renovated. It felt like it might be the town plaza. Things were fairly run down and covered with graffiti in a lot of areas but the people seemed cheerful and the walk was pleasant. We walked the back ways through the city and poked in little shops and eventually ended up in another plaza area. There was a strange statue of a woman riding a chicken, carrying a fork. We walked up to it and laughed about what we thought it could mean, which was about all we could do since we couldn't find a sign or plaque explaining it anywhere. The woman on the statue was naked and Amelia actually made the perverse joke about a naked woman on the "rooster" (substitute the word rooster to get the full effect) and got me laughing pretty hard. Amelia told me she had to go to the bathroom. She actually said, "I need to go to the ladies," and pointed to a bright blue building behind us in the plaza with what looked like another coffee shop in it. It took me a minute to connect what she was saying, but I nodded and took her coffee.

That was it. She was gone. I waited at the statue for 15 minutes and then started to worry. I walked over to the coffee shop, which was pretty full, and looked around. I went back to the bathroom, which was a unisex bathroom. She wasn't there. I pulled up her picture and tried to ask the man behind the counter if he had seen Amelia but he shook his head and shrugged his shoulders. At that point I started to get really worried. Bramble had a direct message option, which was the only means I had to contact her. I sent a curt "where are you?" message, to which I received no reply. I ended up waiting at the coffee shop by the super odd lady on the chicken for two hours. She never came back. I got a message a few days later from Amelia that said, "Sorry Justin. I was in the coffee shop and there was a weird guy who spooked me. I hopped on the Wink pad next to the register of the coffee house and Winked home. I should have messaged you or something, but I was super embarrassed."

Amelia and I had fun but that was the last I saw of her. There was no way I was going to give it a second chance after spending hours sitting in a coffee shop in a country where I didn't speak the language waiting for a girl who had spooked herself into a panic. I figured it wouldn't get much better. My experience is people try to be the best versions of themselves on first dates. People don't want to share their dirty laundry out of the gates. There was a Seinfeld episode where he goes on a date with Janeane Garofalo's character. Jerry thinks she's great because she's just like him, then he realizes she (and he) is pretty annoying and can't put up with her anymore. Amelia would have probably ended up the same.

The third time was the charm. I had nearly given up since the last two experiences were pretty bad, but then I realized I had enjoyed the places and wanted the excuse to see more of the world. I hopped back on the app and picked the next girl on the list. My logic was that the last couple of times I tried to be "selective," but neither had worked out. Time to roll the dice and let fate take over.

I matched with a girl from Singapore. She had an awesome smile, big brown eyes and seemed to be that cool kind of quirky. The Bramble profile showed her in a black tank top with a picture from the oldest character on the Golden Girls, Sophia, and the word savage over her head. I was smiling as I clicked the "ask out" button and began the wait. After she accepted, I found out her name was Luna and we agreed to meet somewhere she was comfortable. That meant a place close to home and somewhere she had visited a few times before. She chose Gardens by the Bay in her home country of Singapore.

There was a Wink Station consisting of about twenty units at the Marina South Pier subway station. I winked into a very clean and fairly empty subway walkway. It was wide with tall ceilings. The walls were clad in dark gray marble and I was facing a large set of stairs with escalators on both sides. The Wink units were set in a corner in a walkway that looked like it led to the train platforms. Clearly the space was not built for Wink units but they had found a comfortable place to set the units and it was accessible. I rode up the escalators thinking about why the station was so empty, and I realized there really wasn't a need for subways when you could wink to the office in an instant. A google search of Singapore before I left told me that Singapore had more millionaires per capita than anywhere else in the world and moving around the subway and to the streets made me feel like I was in a sci-fi city. When I walked out of the station and took a few paces out on a sidewalk that was surrounded by green grass, I spun around and saw the city around me. The buildings were giant and looked like they might have been in the Jetsons. One building looked like three huge towers with a monster-sized surfboard sitting on top. It looked like there was a viewing platform on the surfboard. I used the augmented reality function on my phone and held it to the building. The building was called Marina Bay Sands and looked really cool in the pictures. I decided to visit it at some point. The walk to the gardens took about fifteen minutes. I probably could have made it in less time but I was rubbernecking the whole time.

The gardens were amazing. I had never seen anything like it. There was a mix of modern buildings and nature. It felt like a utopian dream, like if the elves of Rivendell had amazing technology. I met Luna at the McDonald's in the middle of the park, because of course there was a McDonald's there. She was standing in the doorway and matched her photo. She was thin and not very tall with big brown eyes and long black straight hair. She had the same skin tone and some similar features to the Native American Unangan people in Unalaska. The best way to say it was that she was beautiful and maybe a little delicate. I expected her to be timid by the way she looked but I was very wrong. She looked me right in the eye and with a subtle British accent said, "So you're the famous Justin?"

I smiled and said "I must be. Though, I am a little worried about what made me famous."

"Hanging out with me of course." She quipped back and smiled. "Want some chicken nugget things? Then we can walk around the gardens."

"I love those chicken nugget things. Not sure what they are exactly, but they taste good," I said.

"Me too. Love them as long as they don't turn me into a zombie," Luna said and then looked at me with a slight turn to her head that seemed to say *let's see if he catches on*.

"Yeah, I wouldn't want to get cooties," I said back, picking up the reference from the movie Cooties.

"We should be good," she said. "Both of us have gone through puberty. Unless there's something you want to tell me?"

"Nope! We are all good," I said back confidently.

Luna ordered food for us. She did ask me if I like Sprite at least before she ordered one for me. I didn't mind. She wasn't being pushy, just quirky and fun, and I didn't feel any need to be in control, though she clearly did. I thought about how she asked for the date to be on her home turf too. Looked a little like a pattern. Still, she made me smile. She was a treasure trove of movie references and was quick to banter with me.

We sat down with a "Happy Sharing Box A," which was twelve chicken nuggets and eight McWings. I didn't even know that McWings were a thing, but I figured the McDonald's in Singapore had their own thing going on. Luna also ordered a couple Sprites, a small order of fries and every dipping sauce they had. At the table she set the box of chicken in the middle and opened each sauce, setting them up in a line in front of the chicken box so that she could easily access everything. She asked me to sit next to her rather than across. She said, "You can dip with me better that way." I, of course, obliged.

We sat, talking about movies, dipping our chicken in each of the sauces then mixing sauces. It was one of the best times I had had in a while. It wasn't like I couldn't have done the same thing at any McDonald's on the planet, save for the McWings, but there was something about experiencing it with Luna that made it special, different. Luna seemed to treat every moment like it was a memory that she would keep with her and I felt like I was lucky to be part of her story.

We left the McDonald's and Luna treated me to a tour of the gardens. We walked to the "Cloud Forest," which was in a giant glass dome. From the outside, I couldn't get a sense of what I was in store for, and before we went through the gate Luna asked if I had been to the gardens before. I told her I hadn't and she grew an ear-to-ear smile, took my hand and pulled me through the door. She pointed at a structure in the middle she called the mountain. It was a giant mass of plants extending impossibly upward with walk ways sticking out the sides all the way up. I craned my neck to take it all in and felt a chill. The chill wasn't just from the sight but there was a definite cool breeze coming off of a waterfall that fell in the middle of the mountain of plants. It passed over balconies with people walking by. There had to be five or six stories of look-outs and falling water with a walkway all the way at the top.

"Come on!" Luna said as she grabbed my hand again and walked me around to the side of the mountain. Brightly colored plants that had to be tropical lined the walkway and random sculptures were intermixed everywhere which highlighted the strange mix of nature and man under the dome. The sounds of falling water, plants that looked like pitchers, venus flytraps, the fresh smells, and cool air were incredible, but were made better by the joy that Luna was clearly taking from seeing my eyes go wide around every corner. At the top of the mountain, we looked down and I got butterflies in my stomach. I didn't fall off the bridge but I definitely fell for Luna right there.

We spent the rest of the day talking and walking around the gardens. It was one of the best days of my life. The colors were brighter, the sounds crisper, and I felt the day cementing in my memory. I knew I would remember it always, just like Luna. We went back to the Cloud Forest to watch the sun go down and the lights go up. When we left the Cloud Forest the lights of the gardens were beautiful and overwhelming, everything lit up with color and we walked the gardens a second time to take in the entirely new views.

When the night was over, Luna kissed me on the cheek, told me she had to go and asked if we could meet again. I stuttered my way through an "Of course," and waved as she walked out of the gardens and into a car. Downloading Bramble was the best decision I had ever made and Wink Tech was the best thing ever invented.

Justin Skay (2)

Far from Home

We traveled together, Luna and I. We made our way around the globe since there was nothing holding us back. There were Wink Stations all over the globe and the only thing that restricted our travel was the money to buy our way into venues and attractions. The prices had gone way up, like skyrocketed. With the people not spending their money on traveling to places and staying in hotels, their vacation money could be used to experience things, and it didn't take long for the business people of the world to figure that out. Lavish hotels weren't being built, and buildings around the world were converted to attractions.

Luna was concerned about safety. Her father had a pretty tight grip on her and had hammered a fear of the world in her. She wanted to control things as we went but never shied away from an experience once she was comfortable. I was mostly along for the ride since I didn't have money and her father was wealthy and supported her. Luna's dad was our travel sponsor. I should have felt bad about not carrying my own weight. I didn't feel bad because the only thing I cared about was spending time with Luna. There were a few times where I covered things, mostly dinners since the competition for restaurant customers was pretty fierce and prices for food stayed relatively low.

I took Luna to the little bar by my house, the Rat. Things had settled down around Unalaska. The people stopped flocking to town. I assumed they found a new fad to chase, and Unalaska is not the kind of place you would go back to every week to experience again and again. While she was in town, I took Luna back to my house while my dad was away. We watched movies and ate frozen pizza. It was just as much fun doing nothing with Luna as it was walking on a glass bridge over the Grand Canyon in Arizona or taking a gondola ride in Venice.

I still had to go to work at the grocery store but it felt less and less like the place I was supposed to be. Traveling the world and seeing things made Unalaska seem impossibly small, even claustrophobic. Being cooped up in a small town was one thing. The fact that I didn't really have goals in life was another and it felt even more suffocating than where my house happened to stand. Luna had a plan. She wanted to write travel guides. Guides had become really popular. Bloggers were putting together list after list of places and attractions. They curated experiences. Luna had wit and loved to explore. She didn't need money. Those all came together in one place. She started writing little clever stories about the places we had visited. My favorite was a guide she wrote about traveling like a Hobbit. It was genius. She wrote:

"You could live to eleventy-one years old and never have an adventure like Bilbo. A proper adventure needs a few things:

1) Travel companions. You need a Samwise for your Frodo or a Gimli for your Legolas. How can you steal from a dragon without a full complement of dwarves who can sing? You can't. My Sam is a movie nerd I call Justin. The important thing is that your partner be there to keep you moving, even when your legs won't take another step. 2) You have to be ready to eat. Breakfast, Second Breakfast, Elevenses, Luncheon, Afternoon Tea, Dinner, and Supper. They all matter. 3) A little orc mischief.

Now that you have the fundamentals down, it's time to let something Tookish wake up inside you. You're going to see great mountains, hear pine-trees, waterfalls, and explore caves."

Luna's instructions were accompanied by the perfect journey. It only took a day to complete and bounced you from Wink Unit to Wink Port around the world. It started with a Wink to a little town in the Swiss Alps called Lauterbrunnen that sits on green pastures in the valley of two imposing mountains. Then you Wink to the Crooked Forest in Poland where you can wander in tall stands of bent trees that look like the legs of an Ent and you can imagine your own moot. After the forest you head to a Wink terminal that was set up at the Iguazu Falls in Argentina to see a layered set of waterfalls that would put the waterfalls of Rivendell to shame. Finally, you go to the Crystal Caves of Bermuda where you can float on a boat in the clearest water you have ever seen, surrounded by stone dripping from the roof of the caves. We took the trip together after she planned it and it was awesome. She got a ton of hits from devoted Lord of the Rings fans who were looking for something more than a visit to New Zealand to see the movie sites.

Luna's career goals meant a lot of traveling and a lot of Winking around the globe. It was a little disorienting sometimes. We were in Laos once, and I couldn't for the life of me remember what country we were in. I pulled Luna to the side and said, "Where the hell are we? I can't remember where we are." I know I looked panicked but Luna, always in control, never missed a beat. She put her hand on my back and said, "Deep breath. We're in Laos and heading to the ruins in Wat Phu. You look like you saw a ghost." Just her hand on my back was enough to reset me. I realized she was there with me and I knew I could count on her to be in control which allowed me to relax.

At night, Luna would bury her face in her laptop looking for the next cool place to visit. She followed every travel writer she could find. I did wonder in the early days if the followers of the travel blogs were mostly just other travel bloggers "following" posts to build their own portfolio or maybe it was like musicians being the biggest fans of music. Despite my doubts, Luna's following grew. She found a niche and exploited it. Her movie obsession really paid off. She basically started building movie trips that weren't really about visiting the sites where the movies were filmed but were about experiences that were like the movies. Her approach was unique and people really enjoyed it, especially the movie buffs.

Luna's attention to detail was amazing. Before every trip she shared the plans with me in a rambling speech that was closer to a stream of consciousness than a bullet pointed list. She would speak really quickly like if she didn't get it all out in a hurry it would get stuck in her throat and never make it out. It was like a text message with no punctuation. "Here is what I have for our Scott Pilgrim voyage. First, we go to Toronto and visit a park where we can swing on the swings in the middle of a little neighborhood, then to Casa Loma, then to the Sonic Boom record store next to a virtual reality experience where you can pretend to be Mario and run through levels, then we go to a little Tex Mex restaurant for nachos and tacos like in the books, then to a punk rock night club where they do a battle of the bands, and finally to a fancy nightclub downtown. We'll have to see if they feel right." She dragged me along on every trial run. It was awesome. Also, it wasn't lost on me that my first Bramble date was sort of a movie trip, an epic disaster with a girl who didn't really like movies, and my last Bramble date ended up being with a girl who really did love movies and made traveling her life. I guess life is circular like that.

Luna found the perfect name for her travel guides. She called them Flinks or Flinking. It was Wink and flick combined and it had the added benefit of Flink meaning agile and nimble in German. She was able to buy the website too since no one seemed to be working the puns as much as we were. The website had links to her video tours and map downloads with the Wink locations of her travel itineraries. All the maps came with anecdotes and quips. Eight hours a day of "work" was Luna's objective. If we weren't traveling, she was planning, studying or posting. She posted a ton of pictures of us on the trips too which made it our thing, not just her thing. She liked to take pictures of me doing goofy stuff and it seemed her Flink followers did too. After six months of traveling, Luna quit her job, stopped taking money from her dad, and was living off of the Flink income that came from advertising and sponsorships. The whole thing was a dream come true, especially for me since Luna never really pushed me to contribute. I just tried to support her passion and always say yes.

A million followers in, we realized we were getting famous. Especially when interview requests started to come in. At first the requests came from online channels like YouTubers and a few social media influencers. The first big interview was with Project Zorak, a YouTube channel. Project Zorak had turned into everything Wink. They pretty much reviewed all the things people were doing using Wink tech. After their famous interview with Lax and Lad, the two hackers that leaked the tech, they built a big following of people who were eager to see the tech take off and were excited about the possibilities it presented. They cashed in by converting the channel to a Wink hype channel. They had a really solid following. Most of their videos had ten million views. People watched around the world because they liked to imagine a future when everything was made possible by Wink. There would be no borders, no hunger, no repression and a whole lot of money… somehow.

We met with the host of Zorak, Chris Klein, in advance and he said he wanted to talk about what it was like getting a following going and how much work it was keeping Flink going. Luna and I were both nervous but also equally unsure what we should do to prepare. So, we didn't.

Chris had us Wink to his studio in Tel-Aviv. Of course, he had a Wink Pad near the green room of his studio. The studio was converted office space, which was obvious because there were glass windows that looked out at cubicles and conference spaces with long tables and white boards. On the other side of the glass, there were business people wandering around in suits. It sort of felt odd being there since we were in jeans and hoodies. It felt like we had invaded the offices of some New York law firm and were running a pirate radio station.

The green room itself had no windows. There was a wall with a big mirror that had lights going around the edge and a bar top with chairs, presumably for freshening up before your interview. On the wall adjacent to the mirror was a well-worn sofa with a small coffee table. The coffee table had snacks in one bowl and drinks in another that was filled with ice. We raided both and made jokes about the mirror looking like something out of a movie like the Joker or that movie Taxi Driver with Robert DeNiro. Neither of us did much to check our appearance. It wasn't about that for Luna. She was more concerned with the content than her image and it never seemed like the fans much cared, other than the ever-present internet trolls that lurked in every forum or chat space.

Chris called us into the studio and sat us down at what looked like an old conference room table with big microphones sticking out of the center of the table on bendable arms that allowed the mics to be set to any height or angle. It looked like the table had grown arms like that old Kurt Russell horror movie, *The Thing,* where the guy's head grows legs and starts climbing around the room, only the business guy version. The assistant handed us headphones and set us down in seats next to each other while Chris put on his headphones and started testing his mic. He looked over and said, "You both ready?"

"Sure," said Luna and I nodded, fully intending to stay quiet for as much of the interview as I could. Luna would hold court. She was really relaxed and good in interviews.

"Okay! Team we are ready to go live. Give me the countdown." Chris said.

We heard a countdown from ten in the headphones and at zero Chris picked up with what must have been his standard intro for the show after a little music. "Welcome to Project Zorak. Today, we're talking to a couple of Wink travelers who you probably know if you've seen anything about Wink travel blogs, Justin and Luna. They put together movie themed travel experiences and post them out there for you all to enjoy under the name they coined 'Flinking'. Luna, Justin, Welcome to Project Zorak."

"Thanks! It's awesome to be here," Luna said brightly.

"Let's jump right in. You guys met through one of those global Wink dating apps, right? What was that like?" Chris asked.

Luna looked at me, cracked a small smile and said, "Could have been worse. I guess we just got lucky. I hadn't really gone on many dates, and the one's I went on weren't very interesting. I think Justin had it a little rougher than I did." It was clear that Luna wanted me to talk...so much for keeping quiet.

"I had a couple odd dates before I managed to find Luna. It was totally worth it though. Plus, I can totally laugh about them now. For example, one of my dates just disappeared mid-date. I ended up waiting around for hours worrying something bad happened. I must have looked super odd loitering around a plaza in Cuba by myself looking around all the time expecting her to show up and she never did. She did text me the next day to let me know she was okay. Super odd experience." I filled in. I guessed it went over well because both Chris and Luna were smiling at me.

"You have to taste the vinegar to enjoy the sugar, eh Justin?" Chris said and winked at Luna.

"I guess so, though you might argue my date with Luna wasn't the most normal date ever. It was a little weird, but it was definitely kind of amazing." I said and was instantly worried I overstepped and I shot a look at Luna.

Being Luna, she caught my concern right away and filled the air. "What's weird about eating all of the McDonald's chicken?"

It was an invitation and I jumped back in. "It wasn't the chicken, it was the lining up all the sauces in a perfect line and then methodically testing all the sauces separately, then in combination. Actually, it was the best McDonald's experience ever. I recommend the spicy mustard with sweet and sour. Give it a shot."

"Right after this show, we are going for some McyD's," Chris said. "Maybe that's a good representation of what makes your travel blog so popular. It seems like you guys really try to experience it all and then your recommendations are detailed and different from what people would expect. Do you think you bring that weirdness to your work?"

"For sure," Luna said. "I sort of want to figure out the little secrets and nuances of every place we go. I'm not adding much to a traveler's experience if I'm not getting into the weird little things for each trip. I mean, it's our jobs now and we take that pretty seriously. We have to go through things and find the best combination. We have to mix all the sauces. Some will come out gross and some will come out awesome. We get to pass that along."

"Let's talk about Winking. Do you think you would be doing travel writing if it didn't exist?" Chris asked.

"I hope so, but if I am honest, probably not. I mean it sort of changed everything. Didn't it? I would never have met my travel partner. He's a big reason I feel comfortable enough to go out into the world. Also, I can do a monthly travel experience. I could never do that without the mobility we get from Winking. My favorite part is that we can curate experiences that bounce around the globe all in the same day. There is no other way to pull that off." Luna said. It was funny to hear that I made her feel comfortable considering I counted on her for that. I guess it went both ways.

The interview went on like that for a while. It turned out that Chris had taken one of our trips and loved it. It wasn't the kind of thing an interviewer normally did, but he went on about his experience for like ten minutes. He had done our tour for the movie Zombieland and said it felt like following the plot. He actually watched the movie in sequence with the tour and he said it lined up all the way to Pacific Playland.

The next day we got an email from a producer at the Late Show with Stephen Colbert. He saw the interview and had been thinking about asking us to come to the show to talk about our hobbit adventure since he was such a big Tolkien fan. Apparently, he hadn't reached out because they weren't sure how we would do in the interview, but after the Zorak interview he felt good about it. We were slotted for four minutes that would be shown online. We had built a good following, but nothing like we would pick up after our interview with Colbert. We definitely got the "Colbert Bump." We were going mainstream.

Colbert was in a few movies and a lot of shows. We decided to do a "walk in the footsteps of Stephen" tour and reveal it on the show. The thing that made the Wink journeys awesome was the ability to jump all over the place in a hurry. We knew we would need New York where his show was, Chicago where he got his start and Charleston where he grew up. We kicked off the trip in NYC to get a BLT for breakfast, a Colbert favorite, at a deli he slammed for not having enough tomato, then some sight-seeing. Then to Charleston for a swim in the ocean off Sullivan Island and some shrimp and hominy (not grits according Colbert) for lunch. Finally, to Chicago for a hotdog for dinner, since Colbert managed to get the supreme court to weigh on whether a hotdog is a sandwich, then an evening at the Second City improv theater where Colbert performed in his early career. We gave it a shot and it was a pretty cool trip that was filled out by funny Colbert videos. They weren't deep cuts on the Colbert catalog, but it was fun and easy to get set up on short notice.

The Ed Sullivan theater was on Broadway in New York which gave us a chance to wander around and see the city a little before the show. New York was pretty intense just with the density of people, but knowing we were going to be on the show sort of made everything a little duller in the background. I was just wandering around thinking about what it would be like on the show and stressing over how I would do. Stress put the city in the background. When it was time, we went to the theater and hung out in a narrow little room painted white with a black couch, little table and TV on the wall where the show was on for us to watch while we waited our turn. We were the first guests, so we sat through the monologue where Stephen made jokes and bantered with the band. Handlers guided us to behind the stage and led us to the coaches.

"Our first guests tonight are a couple travel bloggers who have recently gained some popularity for a trip they planned around Lord of the Rings. Naturally, I needed to talk to them. Please welcome Luna Poh all the way from Singapore and from Unalaska, Alaska, Justin Skay." Stephen stood up and the handlers nudged us to walk on stage. Stephen greeted us and directed us to the chairs next to his desk. "Welcome! Thanks for making the wink here!" Stephen said.

Luna knew to speak up first and was so natural. She never ceased to amaze me. "Thanks for having us."

"I need to know, right off the bat. Are you really Tolkien fans or have we made a horrible mistake inviting you here?" Stephen said with a wry smile. The audience laughed on cue.

"Oh, we're fans, but I don't know that we can meet you on your level. I can't quote the *Silmarillion*, but I know what it is. Does that count?" Luna said smiling and the audience laughed.

Stephen leaned in and in a voice just above a whisper he said, "So, I hear things on the news and see all the chatter in social media about how dangerous Winking is. I read that it makes men...uh hum," Stephen cleared his throat and continued, "have performance issues shall we say, and that the big corporations are using it to copy everyone's DNA. Not really sure what for, but still, aren't you nervous about how much you use it? I mean, your livelihood is linked to it now."

Luna looked at me, knowing she was going to speak for both of us, and said, "We haven't noticed any trouble with the first one," she said with a wink, "and the second one...I guess they can have our DNA as long as we get to be anywhere, we want whenever we want. Seems like a fair trade. Though, I don't really think they are taking our DNA. What use would it be to them? I mean...did you ever notice how no one in Star Trek ever had a space suit handy. It was like they weren't worried about being in the vacuum of space. The only way that would make sense is that they had become so comfortable with being out there that it wasn't really a worry any more. It was just part of the normal risks they take with everyday life. Wink is going to get there too. We're still just early in the tech." The crowd laughed. It was clever. After the show I asked Luna if she planned that joke. She didn't.

"You must at least think about it. What do your parents think about your gig?" Stephen asked.

I spoke up, "My dad is all for it. He's on boats a lot for work and thinks traveling is an important part of being a well-rounded person. He's a pretty encouraging guy, and I guess you could say he was more into letting me figure stuff out for myself."

Luna shifted in her seat. Stephen looked at her and waited. I know the pause was only for a moment or two but with the lights and the audience the quiet seemed to last forever. No one was talking but it felt like Luna was getting grilled. She timidly said, "I guess...I guess my father doesn't really like it, but he allows it since he isn't able to be home all that much. He works for the government in Singapore and that keeps him away a lot. I don't think he's worried about them stealing my DNA, but probably about my safety."

"Sounds like he has misgivings." Sensing the mood dipping, Stephen did a turn. He smiled and said, "but you don't! Ahh, to be young. What are you kids up to next?"

We told him about the Colbert trip and walked through the details. He told a few jokes and reminisced a little and then the whole thing was done. It was over so fast compared to the build up to it. It wasn't a letdown, but I felt like I would need to go watch the video again to remember what happened. It was a blur.

After the show, things blew up. Businesses started to reach out and ask if we would add their locations to our guides and we took full advantage. We stopped paying for our excursions altogether. We had sponsors and it became a full-time gig. I quit my job at Safeway and dove in head first.

I'm not sure when it happened. Heck, I'm not sure it wasn't always there from our first nuggets. Maybe even before. I realized I loved Luna shortly after I quit my job. All her quirks and gags, her relentlessness, and her constant drive to be in the world. She managed to be tough as nails and vulnerable, which is an odd combo and would likely make her a wicked mother, if we ever got there. She wasn't perfect, but I was pretty sure she was perfect for me. I had become completely enveloped in her. She was the sun, and I was in her orbit. All that added up to me needing to propose.

I am an awkward guy by nature. Extra stress does not help the situation. While I was planning for the proposal, I couldn't seem to act normally around Luna. I was sure she was noticing. She was. She was just cool enough not to say anything. I wanted it to be perfect. Of course, I thought it was a good idea to do it while we were on a trip. We went to tons of places: churches with big arches and cool stained-glass windows, wonders of nature, and strange clubs all around the world, but none of that seemed right for my proposal. I wanted it to be at a McDonald's and, as much as it worried me, I wanted to get it on camera for the fans. We don't really live stream. So, I figured if she said no, I could just take my phone and crush it into little bits as I ran away and hid somewhere dark and alone.

I found a ring. Nothing too fancy. No big stones or anything. She wouldn't have wanted something too fancy, just something small that fit. I kept it in my wallet in case the perfect moment came up and the mood hit me.

After carrying the ring around in my back pocket for a couple of months I found my moment. We were in New Zealand to set up a *Chronicles of Narnia* trip. While there, we were on a local radio station's morning show. The host asked how we met and Luna explained the dating app and our first trip to McDonald's. The radio host said, "Macca's is the best, eh? We love it here. There's a Macca's made out of an old airplane by Lake Taupo. Super cool place. I'm not sure about all the sauces though. I'm partial to just some t-sauce on mine."

I told Luna we had to check it out and she agreed, eagerly. There was a Wink unit right outside the restaurant which didn't resemble a McDonald's. It didn't resemble a building. I was expecting a building with a plane on top or maybe sticking out of the front, but the first thing you see about the McDonald's in Lake Taupo was just a plane propped off the ground a little with McDonald's written on the side and cars parked next to it under the wings. The plane was a commercial plane that I thought was a DC10, painted cherry red and silver. The actual McDonald's was next door to the plane and to get to the plane you had to go inside, order and walk through the play area. There was seating in the plane and you got a good look at the cockpit. All-in-all it was a pretty cool experience. The sauces were a major let down. They only had a couple options and nothing interesting or fancy. Still, that wasn't the point of the trip and my nerves were pretty frayed since I knew I had a job in front of me.

We ordered our food, a pile of chicken stuff to be a little nostalgic. Luna ordered and frowned at the sauce selection. I carried everything, shakily, past the kids in the play area and up the jetway-like steps to our seats in the plane.

We sat, Luna unpacked the food, and I fumbled around in my pocket. I was struggling to get the ring that I had slipped into the little watch pocket of my jeans after I paid for the food. On the other side of the table, Luna struggled with the barbeque sauce. The film over the top didn't seem to want to be pulled off. I offered my hand to take the sauce, she reached out palm up with the sauce container rested on top. As I grabbed the sauce out of her hand, I slipped the ring into the place where it had sat. Luna's face looked a little confused. As she pulled her hand back and inspected what was in it, I said, "Luna, I love you." We both paused and stared at each other for what felt like five days but was probably only a few heartbeats. Luna's eyes began to tear up. I said, "Marry me?"

Tears dripped slowly down Luna's cheeks. She didn't speak. She just nodded her head slowly, never breaking eye contact. She smiled and I relaxed a little. Her hand dropped, open with her palm up on the red table, and she just stared at the ring. I instantly started feeling self-conscious. Maybe I should have gotten a ring with a big diamond or something flashier than a thin white gold ring with a small stone in it. I felt the need to talk to cover the moment. I said, "There's a little diamond in there you know."

"Awe you got me a caharly diamond." Luna answered with a little laugh.

"No, I got it from a jeweler in London." I responded a little defensively.

"A caharly! Cause you 'can hardly' see it." Luna laughed much louder and I laughed too. She loved the ring and I loved her for loving it. The day was perfect.

Justin Skay (3)

Braveheart

I met Luna's family shortly after I proposed. Her father was a Singaporean member of parliament, which they called an "MP." Our first-time meeting was at Luna's parents' house which was huge and really ornate. It felt incredibly formal and I wasn't really prepared. I never really had a meal at home like that before. For sure, there was nothing like it in Unalaska. We sat down at a big table, made way too much small talk, ate dinner in a bunch of courses, and then sat in the "lounge" after and had a "digestif," which was a small boozy drink in a tiny glass. Luna told me later the glass was called a cordial. We talked a lot about politics. Luna's father seemed to fall back on it as a topic of conversation when there was a lull in the conversation. I guess it was because he was comfortable with politics, which didn't seem to be the case with Luna's and my chosen field or really much else happening around him. It struck me as odd that they called their Prime Minister an MP. I thought they mixed up the letters, but turns out the PM is also an MP. Luna's dad thought of him as a colleague, not a superior. The PM is just another MP.

Luna tried to talk a little about how things were going with Flink. We were doing really well and gaining a fair amount of notoriety, but her father didn't follow anything she said. He used the open door from the talk of Flinking to steer the conversation to politics and, in particular, the politics of Wink tech. Her dad said the world political order was changing because of winking. No country's borders were secure and "state sovereignty was constantly in jeopardy." He said there was a lot of talk in parliament about how to legislate the "problem" and they were at an impasse, but solving the issue was urgent and required "brave solutions for which the younger generations may not be ready." I mostly did a lot of nodding and occasionally said things like, "That's definitely challenging" and "It's an interesting world we live in."

Saying I was out of place would be an understatement. I had nothing to add to the conversation, and I was pretty confident I came across like a cliche dumb American. Afterward, I was sure Luna was going to call off the engagement. I was sure her dad would say she needed to find someone more in her league or at least in her social class. Her dad had to think I had no prospects and was just following her around like a lost puppy, which might have been true. It turned out I didn't need to worry about his opinion at all.

A couple of days after our dinner, Luna was away at her parents for a few days to work on an event her mother was putting together for her father. It was some sort of state dinner. I was at home mindlessly watching TV, laying on the couch. While I was flipping, I noticed that every channel seemed to be breaking into news rather than any kind of show I actually wanted to watch. Irritating! I was never a fan of news since it never felt like any of it was good news. I gave up after flipping the channels up and down a few times and I let the news roll for a bit. There was a building on fire, which I callously thought was just another bit of bad news somewhere in the states. Then I heard the reporter say Choa Chu Kang, which I remembered from a conversation with Luna's dad at dinner. I couldn't place what we were talking about or what Choa Chu Kang was. I blame the digestif. A cell phone was always in my hands and I did a quick google search.

Choa Chu Kang was a borough in Singapore, the most densely populated place in the country and one of the most densely populated places on the planet. The streets were filled with high-rise housing that looked like it was from the 70s, all white with maroon accents and a fair amount of green lawn in front.

Choa Chu Kang was nowhere near Luna's parent's house, but I figured it was a text-worthy event. I sent, "Hey, just saw something about a fire in Choa Chu Kang on the news. Pretty crazy. You okay?" Then I went back to watching TV.

"...deadliest fire in recent Singaporean history. The initial assessment by local law enforcement said the fire was started in a lower-level apartment in the twenty-story building. The fire then spread up the floors while The Singapore Civil Defense Force evacuated residents and the fire safety system engaged. Seventeen people are missing and we are being told to expect some casualties. Our experts say, for the fire to spread as it has, an accidental fire is unlikely. The apartments have been built according to modern fire safety standards."

The news was pretty heavy, but seventeen people missing seemed relatively small in the overall scheme of things. We are all a little desensitized to tragedy and I'm sure my feelings would be different if I knew someone in the building. Mulling over how I should be more impacted, it hit me that I hadn't heard back from Luna. It was only fifteen minutes or so, but she never took that long to respond. Something was off. I did that spiraling-out thing where I started thinking things like, "No way she was in that building right? I mean she had no reason to be there. Unless she did. Maybe they were doing something for the people in the building. That doesn't make any sense. I should just text her again, just to make sure. No big deal."

So, I sent another text. "I know there is no way you are in the building fire, but you know me...I worry. Can you text me back just so I know you are okay?" Then I turned back to the TV as a distraction. A *Friends* episode was on which I had, of course, seen. It was the one where they try to poke the guy with a giant poking stick to make sure he is sleeping and not dead. Good episode. Midway through the group moving into poking position the news broke through again. "New developments have just come through about the apartment fire in Singapore. It seems the fire was not started by accident, but rather someone has sent an incendiary device through the Wink portal located on the ground floor of the building. No word as to who sent the device at this time. We will update you more as things progress."

I checked my phone but still no response. I grabbed my laptop, shifted my position on the couch and started my search for more details about the fire. The Flink message boards were a good place to see what people were saying. There was a message from Luna in my direct messages. She said, "Hey, I thought you might be getting worried. My dad took my phone. I managed to sneak on his computer and send this message. Things are crazy here. Everyone is panicked because of the fire. I am on lockdown and don't think I will be able to get away for a while. Check your email (I know you don't normally). I'll send you a message soon. Miss you, Luna."

A thousand tons lifted off my shoulders. At least I knew she was okay. It would have been nice if she'd told me *why* her dad took away her phone, but she was safe and that's what mattered. I messaged her back and told her I would keep an eye on my email and my DMs and that I loved her.

More information came out over the next few days. It turned out there were some political offices on the ground floor of the apartment building that belonged to the People's Action Party, which was the party of the sitting Prime Minister. The offices had a dedicated Wink Pad that was open-to-the-public; the idea being the Party could get some public goodwill by distributing Wink Pads at all of their offices and allowing party members to use them freely to get around the city. No one claimed responsibility for starting the fire, but they tracked the originating pad back to a public Wink Unit in New York. There was a lot of speculation about whether the "firebombing" was politically motivated or if it was just a random act of violence. To my memory, that never really got answered. Still, it put Singapore on ultra-high alert. They shut down all Wink traffic in and out of Singapore the next day while, "they assessed the risk associated with the novel technology." The fire struck a nerve in a country that had suffered some relatively tragic fires in the past. It was especially bad considering how proud the Singapore government was about keeping its people safe and ensuring strict law and order. The government seemed to see Wink Tech as taking away a lot of the control they had over peace in their country, allowing every kind of interloper possible through their front door.

I understood the feeling, my town was overrun for a while and it hurt. Still the reaction to the tragedy seemed a little over the top.

I checked my email on a regular basis after it became the only way to talk to Luna. It took like a week to clear out all the spam, clicking unsubscribe to nearly every email in the inbox out of spite even though I knew the inbox would just get infected with Junk again. Luna only sent one email a day. Apparently, she could only sneak into her father's computer to send messages when she was supposed to be showering since there was no fatherly oversight during that time. I missed her more than I could say and her emails were always way too brief. I never seemed to have anything to say about what I was doing since I wasn't really doing much. Mostly, I was just keeping up with our fan traffic by keeping everyone in the loop about Luna's situation and everything going on in Singapore. There was a pretty big outcry within the Flink community against Singapore's limitations on winking, which of course made sense considering the forum was for people who liked to travel the world by winking as many places as they could in a day. When I sent responses to Luna, I tried to include either the really heartfelt fan comments or at least the ones that made me laugh the most.

Luna's emails said things like, "Did nothing today except listen to my dad pace around the house on the phone and complain about how we have 'become a society made up of people who have no anchor to their homeland' or that 'we are all losing our cultures and the world is becoming an even worse place to raise a child.' He and his fellow MPs are on a culture war bender. I think they see this as their chance to make their place in history, but they are totally on the wrong side. I try to tell them, but they discount my ideas, either because I'm young, a girl, or that my life has been built around Winking for a while. What they don't seem to understand is that our generation doesn't really need borders. Besides, it was his generation who thought up social media and that shrunk the world by a lot. Everything in human history has shrunk the world. Before the internet, planes shrunk it, and then cars, boats, horse drawn carriages before that. Winking is just the next step and it makes the world tiny, which they can't stand. Okay, I better go. I miss you and hopefully this will be over soon."

Days, then weeks, passed as I waited for things to lighten up, but the fire in Singapore stirred up a nationalistic emotion in the population and there was a push towards isolation as a path to safety. Given the history of Singapore, which I'd started learning more about by watching history videos on YouTube, it wasn't too surprising. They always seemed to be at the edge of someone else's ambition. I shouldn't have been surprised when Luna shared that her father was sponsoring legislation to lock down the borders and ban Winking in Singapore. The bill carried ridiculously harsh penalties, limited travel and work visas to a very small lottery and basically permanently extended the existing moratorium that was pushed through right after the fire.

I was always pretty good at convincing myself things would be okay when they clearly wouldn't. When my mom left, my sister was pretty worked up. I told her we would figure it out. We were always good just the two of us and it would just mean more time together. Things weren't going to be easy but I didn't dwell on it. I didn't even really let it in. My superpower is my ability to put things out of my mind. I managed to convince myself that the legislation Luna's dad was trying to pass wouldn't make it through since there were too many young people in Singapore and too many people in the country had seen the value of winking, whether it was business owners, people with family outside the country or people who really like to travel. The government was overreacting, and I was confident the people would recognize it and correct it.

In the third week of Luna's isolation, her father's bill was brought to the floor of parliament for debate. I watched coverage on an American twenty-four-hour news network that clearly had an opinion of how things should go and was watching the results closely. I guess xenophobia is contagious. There was very little debate. Mostly, there was agreement that something needed to be done about the risks that Winking presented. An MP said there needed to be better control over what could or could not be passed through the network and it should be set and monitored by the government. The idea was completely impractical because ninety percent of the Wink units were made in the United States and it would require agreement by US authorities. Given the US was unlikely to make changes just for Singapore, the MP felt the best option was to not permit Winking within the country until better boundaries could be set. The arguments went something like that across all who spoke: "If only they changed x but if x can't be changed then ban it."

The walls were closing in as I watched the coverage. It was becoming increasingly clear the bill would pass. Each minute came with greater certainty that my life with Luna was in jeopardy. I grabbed my computer in the middle of watching a commentator pontificate on the debates and sent an email to Luna. In it, I told her how much I loved her and that I was worried we wouldn't be able to see each other. Since I had no real way of getting into Singapore, my suggestion was she find a way out. Sneak away and try to leave the country. Even as I typed it, I realized I didn't really like the idea of her trying something risky like that alone. I erased it and started over. I told her I didn't know how we would make it work but we would figure it out. The closing was a question. "Any ideas?"

Luna's reply came the next morning during her "get ready" time. It was short. She said, "I love you too. We will find a way. I don't know how, but I need to believe this can change. It feels like a nightmare. We had everything and it all got taken away by an asshole with an agenda. I'm basically on house arrest. I was thinking about running, but I'm not even sure how I could. I'll keep thinking. You keep thinking too."

I did keep thinking. The Flinking message boards were where I did a lot of thinking out loud. It was probably a mistake, but I aired a lot of laundry in the chat. The chat community was my only real outlet, and the participants my only real friends. Loneliness and the thought of losing someone you love makes people do weird things.

I told the fans about Luna's house arrest and about how Singapore seemed dead set on passing the anti-Winking laws. I admitted to being lost and out of good ideas, especially since the Singapore government put a temporary ban on foreign visitation. The only thing I had come up with was to get into Malaysia, specifically Johor, and then swim or boat across the Johor strait. Everything about the idea seemed impossible and amazingly stupid. I shared it with the Flinking community. You can really count on the internet to find everything wrong with an idea. Most of the creativity in the comment sections comes from people trolling. They pointed out how many people drown every year trying to sneak into countries around the world. Someone made a really good point about what I would do when, or if, I got there. It wasn't like I knew my way around Singapore. Plus, Singapore police, Coast Guard, and general civil defense would probably be able to spot me pretty quickly. One of the commenters asked if I like getting my ass spanked with rattan since the punishment for getting caught is six months in jail and at least three lashes with a cane. Then everything went sideways, as always happens on the internet, and the conversation devolved into the value of getting spanked and the best thing to get spanked by. The general consensus was that the best thing to be spanked by was Ryan Reynolds, apparently all genders and sexual orientations agree.

It turned out we had fans in Malaysia who offered to help, which felt like a move in the right direction, but I couldn't figure out how to use them. Even if they could get me into the country, I couldn't get around by myself. I would be walking around Singapore with my phone out for the map; then what would I do once I got to Luna's house? It's not like I could just knock on the door and say "Is Luna here?" like I could for a friend who lived up the street. I'm sure the butler that answered wouldn't just say, "Oh! One moment while I fetch her."

I emailed Luna the next morning and told her that I had the idea to make my way into Singapore to come get her with the help of some Malay fans. She said it was a crazy thought, and she loved me for coming up with it. Her house was like a little fortress with a gate and everything. I am not Rambo, but the idea of me with a cool bandana charging into the house to save her was a dream I had more than once during that time.

There was one fan, RedHatRaider, who had an idea I sort of liked. He said, "Why not do a DDoS attack. We get this in IT security a bunch. You get a ton of people to hit a website at the same time and overload the servers. That causes the site to crash. You could do the same thing. We all show up and flood the country, and there would be no way they could keep up with the amount of people. I looked it up, they only have ten thousand police officers in the whole country."

I liked the idea of a mob of Luna's adoring fans all showing up and knocking down the gates of her house. It brought up images of William Wallace in his war paint preparing to lead his people into battle in Braveheart. I did have to look up DDoS though. It is a Distributed Denial of Service attack which, according to Wikipedia, "is typically accomplished by flooding the targeted machine or resource with superfluous requests." My clandestine plans were making me smarter! I went to bed thinking about breaking Luna out of her prison and when I woke up, got a shock. The number of fans that responded to RedHatRaider's initial post was insane. It hit twenty-six thousand in the first few hours and trickled up from there. It was a spirited back and forth at first then a bandwagon formed in a hurry and fans jumped on to the idea of a formal Wink protest. There was a chunk that was pretty funny. I went by TheSkay in the chat.

RedHatRaider: The point isn't to take over the whole country or anything. I mean to sneak in Justin. Like we all show up, keep them busy with a protest, and he goes and rescues Luna

Hopalong: You mean like in Princess Bride?

RedHatRaider: No…I mean like a guy going to get his girlfriend away from her overbearing parents.

MountainMan: Anybody want a peanut?

Hopalong: Gotta dodge the ROUS's on the way in

PradaPanda: Have fun storming the castle

ALPHAdelta: Do you think they'll make it?

MountainMan: It would take a miracle

TheSkay: Could anyone bring their holocaust cloak?

JakeM8: Whoa! Too soon.

RedHatRaider: For real though, we could do it if we all Winked in

TheSkay: wouldn't a ton of people end up in jail and caned?

Hopalong: You mean like the spanking scene in Step Brothers?

Mr.Anderson: You have to learn there are consequences!

Puggalo: Betting it would be a bit more than a spanking

Logansruns: I could use a good spanking...takers?

Pythonese: Yes, you must give us all a good spanking

UnoBetter: Nope...but I will go get Luna out of Singapore

Alpino: I'm in

Hopalong: I'm your huckleberry. That's just my game.

The thumbs up and positive support in the posts were out of control. I stopped watching when there were two hundred or so people in the thread. People seem to like a cause and maybe there wasn't enough going on in the world at that moment or maybe it is a thing with young people. We just want a cause to get behind and to back up our group, even if we have never met them in real life. We were all travelers, Winkers, movie-heads. We were all Flinkers. Maybe everyone just needed something to do, getting restless without the next quest. The whole exchange made me smile. I love that the group was all ready to back me up and really liked the peppered in sarcasm and contestant movie quotes. They were definitely my people.

I mashed up a few of the ideas from the Flink chat and decided to take a couple of the fans up on their offers. With a little help, I could get into the country without having to swim and I might actually be able to just hitch a ride with a Singaporean fan to Luna's house. I would show up at Luna's door, and talk to her, or her parents, whoever made it to the door first. Maybe her parents would let me at least come visit through more conventional means. Fly to Malaysia and then drive to her house or something. The first trip would be a Wink trip, but I would avoid Winking if it meant seeing Luna again.

The Malaysian fans, Yee and Jia, offered to get me across the border to Singapore. They lived in a city at the edge of Malaysia, just across the strait from Singapore where they were attending University. They went to the University of Reading for degrees in business and had taken an English program at the school. Their English sounded British, but it was perfect (they would have said impeccable). The plan was, once we were in Malaysia, they would call a local friend for a boat ride across the strait, then they would smuggle in a Wink Pad for me. Then, once I was there, I brought in some more fans to kick off the protest. Yee and Jia would be relatively safe once they were across the border in Singapore since they had existing student visas. If the police noticed them as out of place for any reason, they could just say they were there for school which allowed them to take their time to find a good, out of the way, spot to set up the Wink Pad for me.

The larger fan group had settled on a plan; each person would wink into Yee and Jia's Wink Unit with their own Wink Unit and then share the addresses of the newly placed terminal. People could join the protest quickly. Exponential growth would result and overwhelm the system. The only limitation would be the space available to place Wink Units. If our group didn't bring in people fast enough there was a risk of getting caught and the whole thing would get shut down before the attention of the local authorities could be diverted.

I didn't exactly feel good about the whole plan. A bunch of people would be risking a lot just so I could talk to Luna, and the whole movement had started to take on a life of its own. In the fan chats there was excitement and a growing anarchist feel. It might have been all talk or maybe not, but either way, with all the chatter, I wasn't sure we would be able to pull it off. I was sure the Singaporean intelligence services were watching and would cut us off right as we started. There were videos of what it was like to be caned and to be in prison in Singapore on the internet that I started watching more often than I would be comfortable admitting. Some days the videos were comforting and on other days they gave me anxiety attacks. What really got my anxiety going was the thought I might be joined in prison for a visit or a spanking by people who didn't really have any purpose going.

I met Yee and Jia at the Legoland near Yee and Jia's house. They had season passes and Legoland had the added benefit of ample public Wink terminals. We figured there was anonymity in crowds, though, really who would have been watching? When you get the clandestine bug it's easy to think there are people watching everything you are doing when really no one cares all that much. People are more worried about the junk going on in their life, and not the junk going on in your life most of the time.

Legoland was like a little American oasis. If I didn't know I had wandered to Malaysia, I'm not sure I would have realized I'd left the United States. The Wink Units were right outside the ticket purchase gates where people were moving in every direction, like ants who just got dropped into a new aquarium. Some were entering the park; some were leaving and some were winking in and out. I paused after stepping off the Wink Unit and noticed a young couple standing still and smiling at me near the terminal. It had to be Yee and Jia, everyone else was in motion. They noticed me even quicker since I didn't look much like anyone else around.

Yee and Jia were Marvel movie nerds. They both had Marvel t-shirts on when they picked me up. Yee had a Moon Knight shirt with Moon Knight's mask surrounded by moon darts, which he was happy to fill me in on as we drove back to their house to get the finishing touches on the plan. Jia had on a She-Hulk shirt since, as she told me, She-Hulk was a smart and powerful woman who needed her day on the big screen. Some of the characters in the movie Shang Chi were Malaysians which helped the popularity. Also, people in Malaysia apparently even got the movies a week before we did in the US, though maybe not for the best possible reasons. The studio executives decided, at some point, that when movies drop in the US, they can't really control how quickly they get pirated and distributed throughout Asia. To minimize the practice, they release the movies early in places like Malaysia, hoping that people will go see them in theaters. At least that way they can make some decent money on the release before the pirated copies make their way around the continent.

About thirty minutes later we got to their condo, which was in a large high-rise. They were on the third floor of a twenty-story building. The condo was like a large hotel suite, but was very clean and felt homey. The condo complex was really nice too. They had a pool, and we passed a gym on the main floor as we came up. I had an itch to look up how much it cost to live there. With winking, I could really live anywhere and the prices were super reasonable. It was only about $600 US per month. I made a note on my phone to check back when things settled down. It would be pretty cool to have Yee and Jia as neighbors.

I remember thinking about how jet lag must have felt. I didn't really leave the island much until we started winking. It must have been crappy to get to a place you were looking forward to visiting only to be exhausted when you got there and have to waste half a day trying to catch up. Winking was so much better. I was ready to go right when I got to Malaysia.

We all sat down at their round glass-top dining table. It sat four, but was plenty roomy. Jia pulled out a laptop and said, "Well, what first?"

"Can we run through the plan to get into Singapore? Also, I really need to figure out how I am going to get to Luna's place once I'm there," I said. I was feeling a little self-conscious because I should have come up with a plan before I got there. If I am being honest, I lost a fair amount of time just checking the chat rooms constantly to see who would join, and I just couldn't get my head in the game to make a plan. I was used to planning everything with Luna and I couldn't even get started without her.

Yee said, "No worries about our side of things. Jia's uncle has a boat that he uses for fishing. He is going to get us close to shore and we have a little boat that inflates to take us to the shore. We are bringing a portable generator and will connect our Wink pad once we land. Jia and I talked, and we think you should be the first to come over on the Wink and start making your way to Luna's. Once you're moving, we will start bringing everyone else over to distract the police. Jia said that she would bet you would be stuck talking to everyone as they arrived, and you would never get anywhere." I had assumed I was going on the boat with them. It felt odd for them to take a risk without me even being there. Before I asked about being on the boat Yee said, "Also, the less people on the boat the better. It's not very large, and Jia and I have free passage into

Singapore anyway. Going with just the two of us minimizes the risk. We figure we will be able to see any presence on the shoreline and if we get pulled over by a patrol boat, we will have not done anything wrong yet. It seems the safest path."

"Wow. Thanks, you guys. You put way more thought into this than I have. I'm kind of embarrassed." I said, looking down at my hands on the table.

"No problem, my man. Jia and I love this stuff. We have some ideas on how you can get to Luna's too. Want to hear?" Said Yee, his voice was peaking at the end with some obvious excitement. He wasn't lying, they really did love logistical stuff.

"Definitely!" I enthusiastically replied.

Jia pulled a map from a stack of stuff on the kitchen counter, unfolded it and set it down in front of me. It said MTA at the top and a path was highlighted. Jia said, "This is a train map. You can get lots of places by train in Singapore, really good transit system. It isn't even that hard to get close to Luna's place by taking a couple trains. As long as you seem to know where you're going, people may not even really notice you. All you have to do is grab the brown line from Woodlands, which is pretty close to where we will land. You could just get off at Orchard...here." Jia pointed to a circled spot on the map with a pen she was holding in her hand. "Or, you can swap trains to get to the Newton station...here. Both are really good. You will be close enough to walk. The Newton station is a little closer, but it may not be worth the extra complexity."

Jia was talking fast. It felt like she had been saving up the plan until I got there and needed to dump it all out at once. I was overwhelmed. All I could think was that I needed to keep it simple. I said, "I should do whatever is easiest. They didn't really have trains, or really many roads, where I grew up. I don't want to get lost or end up on the wrong train." My self-deprecation drew a smile from Jia which I interpreted as a little bit of pity mixed with the look you give a country bumpkin the first time, they ask about your cement pond. Maybe that was why I loved Luna so much, she was always confident traveling but never made it a thing between us. She would just lead me along, happy to be where she was and happy to be with me, which made me happy to be with her. I was starting to get the impression that her skill in navigating all kinds of cities had a lot to do with where she grew up.

"The brown line to the Orchard exit it is! Then you have a straight walk to Luna's. Let me show you again on the map, and then we can program the route on your phone. Will that help you feel comfortable?" asked Jia in the bumpkin tone.

"I hope so, but I am not sure we can do anything else other than give me an escort. Would that be odd?" I asked, feeling myself falling into the country-boy role that Jia had set out for me. Yee and Jia looked at each other hoping the other would answer first. I could tell I made them uncomfortable. Clearly, they didn't want to split up and had talked about it before I got there. I broke the silence. "That would be odd. I can totally handle it. I mean I am only 'mostly' useless without Luna, not totally useless." I smiled at them both and got an awkward giggle out of Jia. The awkward moment passed pretty quickly when I pulled the map over again and started studying. I asked, "So, it's just straight up the road? No problem. Are there any landmarks along the way that would tell me I'm on the right path? It'd be nice to know when I'm getting close."

"Actually, it's not so bad. Luna's family has a house on Nassim Road, basically at the end of Orchard Road. You are going to pass a bunch of high-rise apartments later in your walk but when you get started there are a few big hotels, a Hilton and a Holiday Inn, and then a big mall on the other side of the street. You just keep walking, and you'll get there. Honestly not bad. Here's a picture of the front gate of the house and of the house itself. Pretty distinctive. Check it out." Yee pushed his phone over to me with pictures. There were those two cool looking statues that were the Chinese dogs that look sort of like dragons flanking a large arched metallic gate. Yee was right. Pretty distinctive.

"Got it. I can spot that. No problem." I said, feeling much more confident. It actually seemed pretty easy, assuming I was able to catch the right train and get off at the right stop. Something I could pull off. Afterall, I was just taking a train in a foreign country where I didn't really speak the language, down a road

I have never been to, and with cops on the lookout for people who aren't from the country. Okay, maybe I wasn't that confident. Still, my pride wouldn't let me admit out loud that I was still worried.

Jia folded up the train map, stood up from the table and walked over to me and said, "You can do this. The path is easy, and you love her. It's like a movie and you are going to Rom-Com your way back to her." She held the map in both hands, did a very slight bow and handed me the map. I took the map and nodded my head. We didn't talk much about the adventure to come after that. We had a quick Chinese takeout dinner, super good. We went to bed early since we were going to get started first thing in the morning. The hope was for Yee and Jia to go out with the early morning fishermen as cover.

Justin Skay (4)

Prince of Thieves

I had trouble sleeping the night before our visit to Singapore. It was one of those nights where you close your eyes, get close, but sleep just won't come. I was slipping in and out of dreams the whole night. I would wake up from some nightmare or another and then doze off again. I remember seeing the clock at 2:15 in the morning and thinking I needed to be up in less than two hours. The thought of how exhausted I would be was going through my head as I finally dozed off. Of course, I fell asleep only to wake up what felt like minutes later to my cell phone alarm. My eyes were scratchy when I rolled out of bed, but I was surprisingly alert and ready to get things started.

Jia and Yee were already up preparing, once again putting me to shame. They were just about to head out and were just waiting for me to roll out of bed to say goodbye so they could wish me luck.

"There is some breakfast in the kitchen. We are going to leave. Stay in touch over text." Yee said.

"We'll text you with the coordinates for the Wink pad once we arrive. Okay? Are you ready?" Jia asked with a big smile. It looked like this was the adventure of her lifetime. I nodded, and they both turned to leave. I could have sworn Jia literally had a spring in her step. At least her enthusiasm made me feel better about getting her help.

I was alone in their house. It struck me almost immediately that they trusted me a lot for someone they never really met in person. I mean, they only really knew me from the online chat rooms. They were going through all this effort for me and had left me at their house alone with all of their stuff. If they were willing to break a bunch of laws for me, I guess it wouldn't be that big of a deal to leave me alone in their house. I had time. We had guessed it would be about two hours before Yee and Jia were able to set up the Wink Pad on the Singapori shore. I used the time to study the map, watch videos about taking the train in Singapore, and send an email to Luna to let her know I was on the way. I figured it was close enough to doing the deed that she couldn't really stop me, and there was a good chance she wouldn't even see the message before I got there. I kept it simple. "I miss you; I love you, and I'm going to knock on your door today. Be ready"

At the two-hour mark, I started to get antsy. Yee and Jia hadn't checked in. I knew there were a million legitimate reasons to be running late, but my mind didn't really let those in. I was one hundred percent sure they got caught with Wink gear on the beach or something and they were on their way to prison or worse. I paced the small apartment, counting off the landmarks in the room as if they were the landmarks on the way to Luna's. There is the couch, the coach is like the Hilton. The coffee table is the Holiday Inn. There is the dining table which is the mall, and if I keep walking and turn into the kitchen, there are the two statues at the gate to the Pohs' house. Or should I call it an estate? I paced and ruminated and wore holes in the vinyl flooring for all of about twenty minutes before I got a text that just said, "made it:1.437522,103.752850"

I texted back with "See you soon" and made my way down to the Wink Terminals on the ground level of the apartment building. I waited in a short line, transferred the coordinates from my phone and stepped on the pad. In a wink I was standing on a shoreline that wasn't a beach of any kind. It looked more like a river bank back in Alaska than an inlet from the ocean. There were trees along the shore and what looked like a river flowing out to the sea. Yee and

Jia were standing between two trees with smiles on their faces leaning in eagerly to see me arrive.

"You made it!" I said.

"We did, and we got you here too." Said Yee. "Are you ready to make your way over? You have a little bit of a walk to get to the train station. Jia said she would walk with you some of the way once we get the message out to the group to start joining us."

"That would be awesome. Thanks." I said, clinging on to the idea of not being alone. I knew I would be alone eventually, but the longer I could be around Jia the better.

Yee said something to Jia in Malay and given her face it was probably something like "Be careful, I love you." It felt like I was intruding on a private moment, and I turned to look at the forest for a minute. Before I turned back Jia said, "Okay!" in a bright excited voice, "Let's go." She walked over to me and tugged my arm. We waved goodbye to Yee and started walking through the trees.

Oddly, our walk through the trees didn't last for more than a few minutes. We ended up right next to what looked like an industrial storage yard. The trees acted as a sort of fence line. In no time at all we were on the street walking through an industrial area. We walked for maybe ten minutes before we ended up in a more urban area with apartment buildings rising all around us. They were tall and everywhere, like its own version of a concrete forest. We got to a street called Woodlands Avenue 3, which sounded familiar from my living room planning session. The name of the train station I needed to pick up was Woodlands. All of sudden I felt confident I was on the right path.

"This is the road. Just a walk down this road to the Woodlands station. Then follow your plan. I am going to head back to Yee and see how things are going with our big distraction. I think you should be at Luna's in about an hour or so. We have a lot of work to do before you get there. How are you feeling?" Jia asked.

"Nervous, but better now that I know I am on the right path. Thanks for everything. You know I couldn't..." Jia interrupted me.

"No time for long goodbyes. Good luck and text us when you get there. Actually, give me your phone." Jia said as she swiped the phone from my hand and quickly fiddled. "There...I made it so I can see your location. If I see you getting off, I will text you. You can do this!" She said as she put the phone back in my hand turned and started to wave goodbye and jog off at the same time.

I waved and got hit by a thousand tons of bricks as I realized I was alone. I stood on the sidewalk for a minute or maybe a few minutes, it was hard to tell. I took in the scene. Cars passed on my right like any normal day. There was no one really walking but there were trees and plants lining the street and sidewalk. I noticed an elevated train track on the opposite side of the street making, me wonder why I wasn't on that train. I noticed a sign that it was the red line, not the right line. I Looked out in front of me. The road was a straight walk as far as I could see with blue signs lining the road saying there was no access to the checkpoint. I had no idea what the checkpoint was, but I was sure it wasn't for me. I started walking and thought about Yee and Jia, hoping they would be okay.

I passed apartment building after apartment building. Some had pink features on the patios or blue roofs, but all about the same height. I was shocked to see that all the signs were in English. It took away the feeling of being on foreign soil, helped me feel relaxed as I walked. Busses carrying people up and down Woodlands Avenue kept passing me, stopping and moving on. I had a feeling I could have taken the bus, but I am sure Yee and Jia thought it was best to not complicate my travel with taking a bus too. Woodgrove apartments came and went, then on to a big open green grass park lined by more tall apartment buildings. I passed the checkpoint where there was a maroon sign that showed a stick figure with his arms in the air and another figure pointing a gun at him hung on a fence in front of a giant white circular set of two buildings. The checkpoint looked ominous so I put my head down and walked quickly. On the other side of the checkpoint the walkway curved through a lane that looked to be merging onto a highway with a blue sign that just said "B K E (SLE KJE PIE)." The feeling of not being in Kansas anymore hit me hard, lighting a fire under my feet. I sped across the street and hurried back to the comfort of more apartment buildings.

I walked past a market, a stadium, people on bikes, people walking, with no one seeming to question that I should have been there. Soon, I was approaching a big building that said Causeway Point, and the street seemed to end. There was a giant shopping mall there where I stopped outside to look at my phone to locate the train station on the map. It looked like it was on the other side of the mall. So, I just stayed along the exterior of the mall and walked around. I passed a store with a TV in the window and noticed a news feed. The broadcast was subtitled in English and had one of those "Breaking News" banners at the bottom that said, "A large mass of people seems to have arrived on the northside of Singapore Island via Wink terminals brought into the country illegally. The SPF have been dispatched to manage the situation." Other people started lingering at the TV with me, so I decided it was best to leave in a hurry. Clearly Yee and Jia managed to get some of the Flink followers into the country. I wondered how many and what was happening to them, but I decided they came here for a reason, to help me, and I wouldn't be honoring that help by standing around waiting to get caught.

The train station was on the other side of the mall, in view of a McDonald's. Seeing the McDonald's reminded me of the first time I came to Singapore when Luna and I dipped in every kind of sauce. I missed Luna. The people sitting at the tables at the McDonald's were easily the most diverse group of people I had ever seen. No wonder I didn't stick out. No one would stick out with that mix of humanity around the city. At that moment I decided I liked Singapore. Maybe it was the McDonald's, maybe it was the people or maybe it was just Luna. In any case, maybe I would try to make it my home after the rescue was done. It hit me like a ton of bricks, would her dad hate me forever for trying to steal her from his house? I started to think it was probably wise to talk to him while I was there, but what the hell would I say? "Sir, I love your daughter and hopefully that makes up for all of your laws I just broke." Or maybe, "Luna is an adult, and it's time you let her be her own person." I was sure that wouldn't get me very far. Well, I had figured everything else out on the fly, I would figure the best thing to say to her father out too.

I made my way to the station and found the terminal where the train was due. I grabbed my ticket at the kiosk and waited for the train to come. I peaked at my phone and checked the news feeds. Nothing had shown up on the US news feeds at that point. I was just finding the news in Singapore when the train arrived, I jumped on and ducked in the back of the train car. The car was surprisingly clean and it was pretty quiet. There was just one old lady with her phone out and on speaker phone as she spoke to someone in what I assumed was Mandarin. Right when I pulled my phone out, I heard someone say, "Aren't you theSkay? Justin, right?"

My heart jumped into my throat and started beating double time. I sat there for a moment, dumbstruck. Someone actually spotted me. Not good. I looked the guy right in his eyes. He was young, skinny, short with glasses on and spiky black hair. He had his finger wagging at me and was looking around the train like everyone should recognize me. I decided saying no would be the best path.

"You must have mistaken me with someone else," I said. That was what they always said in the movies. Though, I wasn't sure it ever worked in the movies.

"Come on man…you are him. What are you doing here?" the guy yelled.

I held my finger up to my lips, "Can you keep it down?"

"Oh sorry, but really what are you doing here?" He said

"Fine. I came to get Luna." I decided I wouldn't be able to keep him quiet unless I talked to him and kept him engaged.

He hopped out of his seat and nudged me over to sit next to me on the little two-seater train bench. He turned to me and did what I could only describe as whisper yelling. "Dude! Awesome. I heard a bunch of people from outside the country were winking into the country right now. You part of that?"

"Yeah, they are trying to help me keep people distracted while I make my way to Luna's." I replied.

"That sounds pretty dumb. I mean it's not like anyone would have noticed just you wandering around. I mean look around you. You don't even stick out. Ha!" The smile on the guy's face went ear to ear. I guess he didn't realize how offensive the comment was. Though, when forced to think about, why the hell did we do it this way? I would have fit in no problem, and now a bunch of people were at risk because I didn't know enough.

"I guess we all got a little carried away." I slumped my shoulders and turned to look out the window. I hoped the conversation would end there, but I had a strong feeling it wouldn't. I was right.

"Oh sorry, dude. I got you! I'll roll with you to her house that way you fit in even more." The guy said it like it was already decided. It appealed to me a little, but the guy seemed like a loose cannon.

"I'm okay. I have a plan." I responded.

"All good! I got nothing going on today. I am going to roll with you. What stop are you getting off at?" he insisted.

I shook my head. "I'm getting off at Orchard then I have to go here." I pulled up the map on my phone and showed him.

"Oh, that's easy. Fancy area, too. Let's go!" The guy was the human equivalent of a manga character. I kept feeling like glint would hit the corner of his eye and a big exclamation point would flash over his head.

"Will you at least tell me your name?" I asked, a little irritated.

"My name is Rui, but I go by Kamina in the forums usually. You should totally call me Kamina and I will call you Skay. It kinda honors the way I know you. Dig it?" Rui was over-the-top enthusiastic.

"Fine Kamina. So, are you just walking with me or what's the plan here?" I asked

"Yeah man, I'll play wing man! yeah!" Kamina said. "Only a couple stops left."

"Cool." was the only response I could come up with.

Kamina took the next couple of stops to tell me about one of the Flinks he went on and how it was awesome. I told him it was all Luna. I was just Robin to her Batman. He didn't really even acknowledge it, and just kept talking.

"Oooh! Our Stop. Come on. Let's roll." Kamina grabbed my arm, and pulled me off the train before I could say anything. He led me to the street and started talking and walking. He was jumping ahead of me to look back while he talked, then he would fall back next to me, get excited about another topic and get in front of me to look me in the eyes again. Kamina was just energy. He was a great distraction from the more nerve-wracking stuff all around me.

After a minute of quiet that allowed me to think through the situation a little more, I turned to Kamina and asked, "You're not thinking of going up to the door with me, are you?"

"Wait! You're just going to walk up to the door?" he answered.

"Not what I was getting at, but yeah. Why?" I spit back at him.

"Cuz, dude! No way you are getting through. You don't know Singaporean parents, bro. They will shut you right down. You need a better plan." Kamina said, hopping ahead of me again. He was moving ahead like the idea actually *made* him walk faster.

"I'm open to better options, but I'm happy with Luna just knowing I cared enough to show up. Her parents can't keep her on lockdown forever, and I want her to know I will be there when this is all over." I slowed my pace a little. Somehow, I was convinced we were moving so quickly we would be at the house any minute and I needed a little more time to plan.

"Oh, bro! They could totally lock her up forever. I mean, more power to you if you want to walk up all hard core like what's his face from *Say Anything*." said Kamina.

"John Cusack, and yeah. That was kind of the point of that moment too, right? He was just making a spectacle to let Ione Skye know he loved her. I'm doing the same thing for Luna." I was starting to get defensive. He had me second guessing my whole plan. "Besides, do you have a better option?"

"Throw stones at her window." Kamina responded.

"I don't know which window is hers." I quipped back.

"Call her cell and tell you're there." Kamina said, letting no air happen between our statements.

"Her dad took her phone away." I fired back just as fast as he asked. We were jousting.

"Pull the fire alarm so everyone runs out." Kamina said with a smile.

"Do they have fire alarms on houses?" I asked.

"Let's stop and get a boombox, and we can play some Peter Gabriel." Kamina's face looked proud of his great, but not very original, idea.

"No time to find a boombox," I said.

"Dress up like a pizza delivery guy and say that Luna ordered a pizza." Kamina threw back.

"Where am I going to get a pizza and costume in the next mile?" I asked.

"Well dang man...there has to be something better." Kamina said, as he huffed out in frustration.

"Seriously though, let me go to the door myself. I don't need a wingman there, okay Goose?" The reference was intended to take the edge off.

"Roger, Maverick." Kamina responded without missing a beat.

Kamina led me straight to the gate and then kept walking with purpose like it took all his will power not to stand at the gate next me waving his hands and yelling at the top of his lungs. Something told me he might just come back and give it a shot if I didn't say something. As he walked away, I yelled after him, "Thanks. Come back in like thirty minutes?"

He turned, bouncing on his tip-toes, and said, "You know it!"

I was basically alone at that point, standing at the gate and conscious they must have a camera in the bell that was next to the gate that rang the door. I straightened my clothes which all of a sudden seemed incredibly shabby, ran my hand through my hair and took a deep breath. I pushed the white button on the metal pad and waited. A moment or two later a tinny voice came over the pad and said, "How may I help you?" in a thinly accented English voice.

"Um, I would like to talk to Luna, please. This is Justin, her boyfr...er...fiancée. You probably remember me." I said, and stupidly waved my hand as if whoever answered could see me. I assumed it was the butler, but the butler didn't talk much when I was there last and the voice was so tinny on the microphone there was no way to know. It hit me like a ton of bricks at that point, it could have been Luna's father and my casual tone would not help me get to see Luna. I threw in a "Sir" sheepishly and far too late to flow with the rest of my statements.

"Luna is not available." The intercom said flatly.

"I am okay waiting. Can I come in and wait? I came a long way to see her," I said.

"I am afraid that is not possible. You may call her via the telephone when next she is available. Thank you and good day." responded the voice.

"No! That won't work! I need to see her." I said yelling much louder than I had intended.

"I am sorry, young sir." There was an audible click like a phone hanging up.

The finality of the conversation left me in a panic. I skipped the intercom and just started yelling as loud as I could. "Luna! I'm here. I love you. I miss you. Find a way out here!" I waited for a few moments and yelled again, "Luna, please." The seconds felt like an eternity. Looking at the door through the gates in front of me, I felt my shoulders sag and my will give in. Lowering my head, I took two steps backward until I was at the edge of the street and the driveway. Looking from side to side I realized I was alone. There was nothing I could do. I thought about hopping the fence. Maybe all the people that Winked in were keeping the police busy enough that when the house staff eventually called for help, there would be no one to show up. A little wave of depression set in, and I started thinking about what would happen to Luna if I jumped the fence. I was hoping I hadn't already caused a bunch of damage, but jumping the fence and rushing the door would probably make things worse. My gesture of love could turn into a home invasion that made it so I would never see Luna again. I decided I did my best, and turned to walk back the way I came.

How was I going to explain to the Flinking group that all of their effort and risk resulted in nothing? Afterall, I could have tried harder, pushed harder, scaled the fence, pushed my way onto the grounds. Why should they be the ones taking all the risk? All the thinking in the world wasn't likely to make me turn around and try, but I did pause. That's when I heard a shuffling at the front door.

The latch at the door made a little noise, like half opening. Then there was a small knock on the door from the inside. The quietness of the street got my attention for a moment. It reminded me of home a little. My tiny, little village with barely any people and this giant metropolis with more people per square foot than nearly anywhere on the planet were somehow the same. The world was tiny again and my heart ached for Luna. I started walking back to the gate listening keenly. There was more shuffling and a rattling of the door knob. The door burst open and I saw the back of a man in a suit with his arms spread wide across the opening of the door.

"Let me out! You aren't my father. If you put a hand on me, you are totally getting fired." It was Luna. I saw her duck her head under the butler's right arm pit and try to squeeze through the door. The butler shifted his weight to that side and trapped her at the shoulder. Luna grunted loudly and said, "Get...out...of...my...Way!" and shoved with all her might. The butler, who was already in an awkward position, was pushed off balance and flopped flat on his butt on the stoop. Luna came running past.

It's a bit silly to say, but my heart jumped. Like literally jumped. I had to cough to get it back on track. Luna ran to the gate and I stared, dumbfounded for much longer than was reasonable. She got to the gate and reached her hand through the bars like she was in prison. I ran up and reached both my arms through and hugged. It was bliss for a flash before the butler regained his footing and ran down to pull Luna back.

"Leave her alone!" I said instinctively. The butler ignored me and pulled at the back of Luna's shirt. She tugged away and sprinted back up to the house. "Where are you going?" I yelled.

"The gate!" she yelled back, and before I could understand what she meant, she was through the door and the gate creaked. It began to open as the butler turned to me and he braced for a coming conflict that I wasn't ready for.

Luna was coming back down the drive as I squared off with the butler. Out of nowhere, I heard footsteps running on my left side. I turned and saw Kamina running full tilt towards me, then past me. I watched as he hauled his arm back and punched the butler in the face mid-run. It was a hard hit that made a thudding wet noise. The butler stumbled back and passed out on the ground.

"What? You weren't going to do it..." Kamina said.

He was right, as much as I would like to think I'm the kind of guy who would knock out someone because they were in the way of me reaching my girlfriend, that wasn't me. Also, I wasn't sure it was wise in the long term. Either way, I ended up with some deniability. I could always say it wasn't me, and it would be the honest truth.

"Okay, I wouldn't have decked him. Where did you come from anyway?" I said, attempting to move the conversation away from my generally soft nature.

"I heard yelling. Thought you were in trouble so I came running. That was some superhero shit, wasn't it?" Kamina said excitedly. He was really proud of himself.

"It was definitely some kind of shit." I said, laying on the snark pretty thickly. I mean, I just met the guy and he was fighting my battles. It was my experience that people like that were dangerous.

I looked down at my arm as something landed on it, Luna's hand. I had momentarily forgotten she was right there while I dealt with Kamina. Grabbing her hand, I turned to her and hugged her hard.

She pulled back after a moment and said, "Justin, what are you doing here?!" She was a little exasperated, but I could hear a hint of happiness underneath. Later, she would tell me that it felt like Robin Hood coming for Maid Marian. At that moment, she was still peeved about the mess all around her. I had just been yelling at her door, she fought with her butler and then watched as a total stranger knocked him out.

Conscious of how dumb it sounded, I said, "I came for you," like that was both obvious and smart.

"I caught that. Jeesh." Luna replied with a heavy sigh. "Well, what now?"

"No clue." I smiled and continued, "I didn't think that far ahead. Should I have?" I was being peevish.

"Yeah! I can't just take you inside," she said.

"Hey wait, where's your dad. I assumed I would have to fight it out with him. Not like actually knocking him out, but you know...with words." I nodded over to Kamina.

"He's gone. He had to go to work because..." Luna paused and the space got heavy. She burst out with, "BECAUSE YOU INVADED OUR COUNTRY!" She lifted her arms and slammed them down through the air to her side. Still, my heart said she wasn't really mad. She had a little smile hidden in there.

"Oh, come on. It's only a few friends from the Flink. I wouldn't call it an invasion." I said with a little smile.

"Wow, you are sadly behind the times. Come on." Luna grabbed my hand and started pulling me down the street back the way we came. I turned to look at Kamina who was quietly watching the scene like it was a movie he couldn't wait to see reach its climax. It was a little creepy but I was happy he was quiet.

"Come on, Kamina." I yelled.

"You don't have to tell me twice, bro." Kamina snuck a glance down at the butler on the ground and started to jog over to me and Luna. "Man, I musta hit him pretty hard. Shouldn't my hand hurt or something? Never did that before."

"It probably will later," I said.

Luna tugged me all the way to a little restaurant down the street, and I explained Kamina and the train on the walk. We sat and ordered some food and some ice for Kamina, just in case his hand did actually start hurting. We were just a few kids out for some food. Nothing special to look at, or at least that seemed to be the hope.

"Okay, here's the deal. Last I saw on TV, there are thousands of foreigners here. They started to march. Some had signs saying things like 'Free Singapore' and 'Winking is a Right'" A bunch of Singaporean kids and some not-kids started marching with them. It was out of control. I think there's a TV here or maybe we can get something on our phones." Luna said as she sifted through her pockets for her phone and looked around the restaurant at the same time. Of course, she didn't have her phone, since her father had taken it. Habits die hard. She spotted a TV Near the kitchen. "There. Let's go over there."

Luna stood up. Kamina and I followed. She sat down at a table closer to the TV. The waiter noticed and walked over looking a little frustrated, dropped off some drinks, ice, and plates with silverware. When I looked around, everyone was listening to news of the "invasion" but the channel was on a commercial break. When the news came back on it was playing in a language that wasn't English. It sounded like Malay or something similar. The newscaster was speaking quickly with a square box of graphics over her shoulder that had a picture of a group of people marching down the street. Some people were carrying signs but most were just walking looking intimidating.

"What is she saying?" I asked Luna.

"She's saying that the number of people marching towards the capitol building is still growing." Luna replied without taking her eyes off the TV.

"Did she say how many people are marching?" I asked. My nerves made my voice pitch up at the end like I was just starting puberty.

"Nah, Dude. Nothing yet." Kamina said nonchalantly while he stared at the TV with the same intensity as everyone else who could clearly understand what the newscaster was saying.

A woman at the table next to me gasped and turned to the man she was with. She grabbed his forearm, which was resting on the table. He absently put his hand on her hand and kept watching the TV

"This sucks," I said, folding my arms in frustration. "What did she just say?"

"She said they aren't sure how many people are protesting, but the estimates exceed fifty-thousand at this point." Luna said absently.

"Really?!" I swallowed hard and asked, "How is that possible? There was only like a few hundred Flinkers planning to show up and make a little noise."

"Well, clearly more showed up. Hush for a minute while I listen. There is some food here, just eat." Luna said, pushing a plate of food at me without looking up. She managed to dunk part of her hand in the sauce which she licked off, all the while staying focused on the TV. Meanwhile, people around the restaurant were discussing details of what was being said in worried tones, but in languages I didn't understand. It was like being alone in public which I didn't realize was possible.

I pushed the food back and forth on my plate for a minute, tried to take a bite and realized I couldn't eat. I felt like a kid in the waiting room while his parents were waiting on a diagnosis of something serious. "Luna, what are they saying?" I pleaded, looking at a couple at a table to the side of us who were talking intently and not touching the food that was sitting in front of them.

"Okay." Luna said and turned to me from the TV "It started with just a few people, the international news broadcasted the protest, and more people started showing up from all over the place, each carrying an extra Wink unit that could be used to bring another person into the protest. It happened so fast that no one seemed to be able to stop it. They still can't stop it. People are popping in all over the place. It's like six degrees of Kevin Bacon or that scene from Wayne's World, where they tell two friends, and they tell two friends, and they tell their friends and so on and so on." Luna paused. "We need to get over there!"

"Holy crap! Did we do this?" I said.

"We?" Luna said with a wry smile.

"Fine...Did I do that?" I said in my best irritating Urkel voice.

"You totally did that. YOU TOTALLY DID THAT!" Kamina said and jumped out of his seat. "I'm going. Are you coming?"

Not one to miss an adventure, Luna grabbed my hand, pulled me up and we were chasing Kamina before I could say anything. I remember actually thinking that Luna and I could just Wink back to my house and be done with it all, but when Luna had a plan, I had no real chance of stopping her. You can't really be mad if one of the things you love about somebody gets you in trouble sometimes. Afterall, I did sign up for the adventure.

Kamina led the way down a side street. It was all a blur to me but we must have been pretty close to the protest because it couldn't have been more than a mile or so worth of walking before we found ourselves in the middle of a giant crowd of every kind of person. The signs were something I hadn't really noticed in detail while I was watching the TV. They were in every language. I saw Spanish, French, Mandarin, Arabic, and a whole lot of English. The crowd made noise but it wasn't noisy. It was oddly peaceful in the line. No chants were going through the crowd at that point which might have been a function of all the different cultures melting together into one.

When the chanting did eventually start, it was in English and we chanted along with everyone else. We would say "We are here to say, you can't take winking away" and then other protestors would respond with "Winking is a right." It was a little off tempo and slightly cheesy, but everyone seemed to get into it. I remember thinking that most protest chants sound a little lame when you really think about them, but it wasn't about being cool. It was about getting noisy, being heard, and making sure the freedoms we all achieved weren't taken away. Not anywhere. With Winking, we had a real chance of preventing restrictions that were wrong by mobilizing a whole planet's worth of activists. It wasn't until later that I really sat and thought about what that could mean. When something really divisive, something that split a population right down the middle, was up for the same Winking treatment and protestors from both sides showed up it would burn down cities and cost real lives but that wasn't in our heads that day. We just wanted to keep Winking alive for all.

We marched all the way to the parliament building. At first, everyone stood in front of the building chanting. It was peaceful and energizing. I felt like I was part of something really meaningful, and I was doing it with Luna right next to me.

We were standing next to a giant palm tree with a little covered bus stop next to us as people pushed their way to the white gates at the front of the building. The crowd pushed and the gate creaked. Someone showed up with a pry bar, then another and before long the gate was down and we were making our way to the front door of the building itself. The crowd pushed its way through the doors and we flooded into the parliament building. The protestors spread out like water being spilled on the floor. There were people going in every direction all at once. Luna, Kamina and I ended up on the second floor and looked out on the crowd. It was immense. It stretched on forever. I was sure there were more than fifty thousand people.

We occupied the building for quite a while. Everyone sort of just settled in after the first hour or so. It was oddly communal. Food managed to get pooled and circulated. People filled water bottles in the bathrooms and we met a lot of really amazing people. Some were Flink fans but many many more had no idea who we were. The sun went down as we looked out through the second story windows. Police were surrounding the building and eventually the military too.

After nearly twenty hours of sitting in the parliament building, a few people started to leave, then a larger group, and eventually the whole crowd dispersed. Why people made the choice to leave was a little bit of mystery to me but we were confident the point was made. We could take over at any time and that meant that the laws had to change.

I noticed there were Wink Pads laid around the building that people must have brought in with them which made a convenient way to exit without getting pulled in by police or military. It was literally easy come, easy go. Luna and I said goodbye to Kamina, exchanged information so we could talk again later and winked back to my house.

We found out later that over one hundred and fifty thousand people had shown up out of the blue from all over the world. It happened with a few and grew exponentially. It went from four to eight to one hundred in a matter of minutes. Then to one thousand, then to ten thousand then one hundred thousand. I did the math that it only took about twenty doublings to get that many people into the country at once. The Parliament met a few days later and decided, under protest, that it was best to attempt to allow the tech but put some rules in place and called for better tracking and foiling of Winking.

It was the first step towards governments all around the world realizing they couldn't control the whole world individually. More effort was spent within the UN and eventually a singular world order. Afterall, no single country could defy the people of the world. It would have to be the same laws for everyone or no laws at all.

Also By Ian Arco Cooper

Fools Despise Wisdom

Fools Despise Wisdom is an exploration of atheism through the eyes of an author who is not a scientist or philosopher. Cooper takes readers through his version of atheism with reasoned arguments and unique points of view. The goal of the book is to help advance understanding of the "average" atheist, not to change minds or contribute to cultural divides.

Made in the USA
Columbia, SC
20 January 2024

1934d095-bee3-4d72-8a91-b2ba26f3d9a8R01